D1526482

This book, *Stefan's Destiny*, is dedicated to my
special friend, Michael DuQuette, who is the
inspiration for
Michael DuKane, the artist in the *Destiny* series.

Sue & Robert —
thank you for being my friend!

STEFAN'S DESTINY

Rosemary Babich Gard

Rosemary Babich Gard

BookLocker

Published by BookLocker.com, Inc., St. Petersburg, Florida.

Printed on acid-free paper.

The characters and events in this book are fictitious. Any similarity to real persons, living or dead, is coincidental and not intended by the author.

BookLocker.com, Inc.
2019

First Edition

CHAPTER 1

Chicago, September, 1915

The slender, handsome man wandered about the Marshall Fields store in Chicago, waiting for his wife who was being fitted for a gown.

He was very fashionably dressed in a lightweight, brown suit. He wore a felt homburg hat which brought attention to his startling blue eyes. His mustache was nicely trimmed.

His gold watch chain held a gold pocket watch safely in his vest pocket.

A beautiful, gold-headed walking stick was held in a hand wearing a large, gold ring bearing his family crest.

As the man casually wandered through the beautiful store, he found himself in the store's art gallery. In front of the entry was a poster depicting a bearded man whose name was Michael DuKane. It read:

SEE THE BEAUTIFUL PAINTINGS
OF NEW ORLEANS WOMEN

Still wearing his hat, the attractive man walked into the gallery. The walls were filled with portraits of various sizes, all of beautiful women.

The man stood in front of a long painting of a red-haired woman. He studied the face. It was as if someone from his past was looking at him. Of course, it couldn't be Katya. She had died before he came to America. The woman in this portrait was wearing a pale blue floor-length gown. His cousin would have been wearing a peasant skirt and blouse, he thought. Still...the resemblance was amazing. As he slowly walked though the gallery looking at the paintings, he was impressed with the display and noticed that some of the paintings had a gold dot on the frames, indicating they had already been sold. He looked about to see if the artist was in the gallery, but he only saw a salesperson.

At the far end of the gallery was a painting featured on an easel. It stood apart from the other artworks. There, on the canvas, was a stunning portrait of another red-haired woman, her hair in the style of a Gibson girl. The sunlight caught her beauty, just as the artist had intended.

Staring at the painting, the man's jaw dropped. He swayed slightly as he recognized the woman. How could it be?

Count Vladeslav was staring at a painting of the wife he had left in Zagreb and then, had ignored at the Gary Hotel when she had followed him to America.

CHAPTER 2

Coralynn DuKane watched with some excitement at the busily working staff in the Marshall Fields Art Gallery.

Pretty Coralynn stayed close to the windows, wanting to stay out of the way.

She smiled at Michael, watching him as he spoke with the men deciding how best to display his paintings.

Today, Michael was wearing a tan-colored, long-sleeved shirt with a mandarin collar. He never wore shirts that needed to be tucked into his trousers. At his neck hung a beautiful amber brown necklace, one of many necklaces he owned.

His shoulder-length hair and beard had been nicely trimmed in the men's salon in the store.

Coralynn's dress was from the Ladies' Department on the fifth floor of the very large store. Her white dress had a square neckline and a slender, ankle-length skirt. A pale, pink panel on each hip starting at her waist was knee length. Her pink shoes with pointed toes and gold buckles were gifts from the store.

Coralynn smoothed her light brown hair and felt the bun at the back of her head held in place with large tortoise shell hairpins.

This trip from New Orleans to Chicago was much better than she had expected.

Coralynn was 28 years old and in New Orleans, though no one said it out loud, she was considered an old maid. Chances of finding a husband were slim, since everyone in their circle of friends knew her father had been in prison for stealing.

She was a pretty woman with brown eyes and a warm smile.

She and Michael had known each other for many years, but never had dated.

Coralynn remembered the lunch at Galatoires in the French Quarter where Michael proposed to her. It wasn't a romantic proposal, but more of a business arrangement. He felt he needed a wife to be with him in Chicago and she needed to get away from an unhappy life in New Orleans.

Now, looking out the gallery window, she was remembering his words at that lunch.

He had said softly and seriously, "I would never do anything to humiliate or embarrass you. It will be on your terms. Whatever you want of me…or don't want of me."

Confused, she had asked, "What are you trying to say?"

He replied, "I want you to marry me and go to Chicago with me or anywhere else we might go."

He nervously added," I will treat you with all the respect I have for you. The marriage will be on your terms. I will make no demands. If ever this arrangement should change from a business arrangement to something more, it would be your decision."

And now, here she was in Chicago at Marshall Fields on State Street. There were 13 floors of merchandise, along with a lovely dining room with a fountain, an art gallery, and an antique room. Beautiful things that no other stores had were offered at Fields.

All of the saleswomen wore simple black dresses with white collars and cuffs. The only jewelry the women wore was a small, round brooch with a retractable chain which held a small, gold-colored pencil. The store conveyed elegance along with the most polite and proper service to the customers.

Coralynn had not been to all the floors of the store. Earlier, she had walked along the balconies surrounding each floor and looked over the side with wonder at the colorful spectacle below.

There was some excitement in the art gallery as a petite woman entered, followed by a young man who was carrying a wooden tripod under one arm and a case in his free hand containing a mahogany camera and a plate holder.

Mr. White, who was in charge of the gallery and was the man who arranged for Michael to have a show in Fields, came hurrying across the room to the woman.

He was pleased to see her and excited to have her take pictures in the gallery.

"Oh, Miss Edda," he said, "we weren't sure you would return in time to photograph this event."

She smiled warmly at Mr. White, extending her hand. In her lovely French accent, she said, "I came as soon as I got word about this show."

"How was it in Ohio?" he asked.

"Very nice." she replied, while watching the young man setting up her camera equipment.

Looking back at the always elegantly-dressed Mr. White, she said, "Taking pictures of the West Side Marketplace in Cincinnati was a challenge, but I think we got it done. I won't know until the glass plates are printed."

Edda turned away from Mr. White and went to the wall of paintings on display. She was a true artist who did not follow fashion. Like Michael DuKane, she had a style of her own. Her dress was a simple, straight brown garment, ankle length. Where Michael did not follow the fashion of short hair for men, Edda also did not follow the fashion of the time. Instead of long hair in a bun; her hair was short, with a wisp of hair across her forehead.

Fascinated, Coralynn watched from where she was standing near the windowed wall. She saw Michael approach Mr. White, who appeared to be introducing him to the photographer. To her surprise, Coralynn saw Michael, take the photographer's hand politely touching it to his lips.

9

Now moving closer, Coralynn heard Michael and the photographer speaking French. Of course she realized Michael spoke French since that is where he was born and spent most of his younger years.

Mr. White, in shirt sleeves and a dark blue-patterned tie, noticed Coralynn. He went to her, taking her by the elbow, and guided her to where Michael and the photographer were talking. He said, "Edda, may I introduce you to Madam DuKane."

Michael said in English, "Edda, this is my wife, Coralynn."

Edda took Coralynn's hand in hers and said, "Oh, you are lovely. I must take a picture of you and Michael together."

Before Coralynn could reply, Michael interrupted saying, "Edda is the official photographer for Marshall Fields. She will be photographing the publicity pictures and those for the exhibit programs."

Coralynn smiled warmly at the pretty woman and extended her hand.

Edda took Coralynn's hand, smiling in return. Before the women could talk, the young man setting up the camera called to Edda, who excused herself and went to him.

Michael guided Coralynn to a soft chair which was along an inner wall. When she was seated he said, "I hope you won't be bored. I have to work with Edda. She will be taking pictures of me and some of the paintings."

"Go ahead." said Coralynn, "I will be fine."

She watched as Michael went to where Edda was positioning the tripod, checking to see that the folding camera was extended and that the focus was properly dialed.

To Coralynn's surprise, she saw Edda touch Michael's amber necklace. Edda said something and then Michael touched the gold brooch which was pinned to the dress near her shoulder. The two of them were behaving as if they had been long time friends and not just introduced.

At Mr. White's request, a small table was brought to where Coralynn was sitting. On it was a silver tray with assorted small sandwiches. The assortment of finger sandwiches was made up of egg salad, chicken salad, and ham salad. Instead of lettuce, in each tiny sandwich there was a very thin slice of cucumber. A pot of tea and a pitcher of ice water were on the tray.

Coralynn caught Michael's attention, indicating there were sandwiches. He shook his head no to the sandwiches while listening to Edda as she told him how she wanted to photograph him.

While munching on the finger sandwiches, Coralynn watched with great interest the interaction between Michael and the charming photographer. This was the first time Coralynn had seen Michael engage in conversation with a woman as he was doing now. The charming Edda was positioning Michael against the wall alongside one of his paintings. She went to the tripod and looked into the lens of the camera. Not pleased, she went to Michael, turned him slightly so he looked at a painting. She then straightened his shirt, adjusted a sleeve and even smoothed his beard.

Coralynn stopped chewing her egg salad sandwich. She was interested in how Edda and Michael worked so well together. He behaved as she had never seen him behave before. She had never seen him work with a woman.

Coralynn studied her husband. Why had she never noticed that he was handsome? She remembered how, always, she thought his style of dress was not appropriate. Yet, this woman who had never seen Michael before, seemed to find him interesting.

Coralynn could hear Edda speaking to Michael in French. This bothered Coralynn because she wanted to know what Michael and Edda were saying to one another.

Mr. White came and sat in a chair next to Coralynn. He looked so very pleased watching Edda at work. He said, "I found her in a store in New York."

Coralynn looked at him, a little confused. He went on to explain, "Her pictures of hats and shoes in the store windows grabbed my attention."

He helped himself to a chicken salad sandwich.

"How did you find her?" asked Coralynn.

He finished chewing and swallowed before answering. "I went into the store and asked everyone who the photographer was. None of the salespeople knew, so I went to the business office of the store. And it was meant to be." he said, "Because there she was with a stack of photos in her hand."

Mr. White's secretary came to him saying he was wanted on the phone. He excused himself and was gone.

Coralynn watched as Edda, laughing, had Michael stand in front of a painting of a woman holding a huge bouquet of flowers. Edda was laughing because Michael was pretending to be picking the flowers from the painting.

Mr. White was almost running when he approached Michael. He said something to Michael and the two of them hurried to the office.

Coralynn wanted to follow them, concerned why both men were almost running to the office at the back of the gallery.

Edda came to Coralynn. She took Coralynn's hand leading her to the wall of paintings. Coralynn allowed Edda to guide her to the wall but kept looking back at the closed office door.

To her assistant, Edda said "Move the camera back. I want to take a full body shot." To Coralynn she said, "Stand in front of this painting."

Edda stood back and studied Coralynn, who was standing nervously next to the painting. Edda turned away and went to the table where the tea and sandwiches were. She picked up a cup and saucer. Handing them to Coralynn, she said, "Turn toward the painting with the cup and saucer in your hand." Edda went to the camera, looking through the viewfinder to study the composition. Not satisfied, she said, "Turn to the right, as if you are studying the painting. Good, good, now with one hand hold the saucer and with the other place your fingers on the cup handle."

Back at the camera, Edda, looking into the lens, said, "That's good. Don't move. Keep your head still…no, lift your chin just a tiny bit. That's it! Don't change your expression. Stay still." Edda pressed the rubber ball which activated the shutter of the camera.

Coralynn saw a very nicely-dressed man walk up behind Edda. He was quite attractive, wearing a tan gabardine suit with a dark brown tie over his white shirt. His brown leather shoes were the modern lace type and not the button high tops.

His hair was parted in the middle and smoothed back. Coralynn could see his admiration for Edda as he looked at the photographer.

Surprised and pleased to see him, Edda said, "Oh, Edward, is it that time already?"

"I know, I know." said Edward, smiling. "You always lose track of time when you are working."

Edda took Edward's hand and led him to Coralynn, saying, "Coralynn, this is my good friend, Edward Barnes, he is in charge of all the publicity for Fields." To Edward she said, "This is the artist's wife, Coralynn DuKane."

He didn't take Coralynn's hand, but bowed slightly saying, "We are looking forward to a very successful show of Michael's paintings. With Edda's pictures, the newspaper publicity, and these beautiful paintings, we are expecting a successful event."

Before Coralynn could reply, Edda said to her assistant, "Pack the glass negatives carefully. I must leave now. You know where to put everything."

Michael and Mr. White appeared just in time to say goodbye to Edda, her face seemed to glow as she introduced Edward to Michael.

Still standing against the wall, with the tea cup and saucer in her hand, Coralynn became aware of the fact that she was smiling, pleased to see that Edda appeared to have a man of her own.

Mr. White, looking not a bit tired from a busy day dealing with all the details of preparing for Michael's art show said, "You may as well call it a day. The store will be closing soon."

As he said this, a woman's pleasant voice could be heard over a loud speaker announcing, "The store will be closing in fifteen minutes. The store will be closed tomorrow, Sunday. Thank you for allowing us to serve you and please come again."

Edda's young assistant had already folded the tri-pod and packed away the glass negatives. He was now folding shut the mahogany box camera careful to protect the glass lens.

Mr. White's plain elderly secretary appeared carrying Coralynn's lightweight lace shawl and her small white leather clutch handbag, saying "Good day, Mrs. DuKane."

Coralynn stood watching the activity as the workers in the gallery were hurrying to leave. Michael came to her side, after shaking hands with Mr. White. He took her hand saying, "Let's go to the hotel. I think I am tired."

Coralynn and Michael walked out of the store onto Michigan Avenue, among the crowded stream of employees. A man was standing at the door watching to see that the bags in the hands of the departing employees had the proper tags affixed to show the items had been paid for.

Waiting for a taxi, Coralynn asked, "Are you going to tell me what the phone call was about?"

Instead of a horse-drawn hansom carriage, Michael hailed one of the new Yellow Cabs, manufactured in Chicago.

Settled inside for the short ride to the Drake Hotel, Michael said, "The call was from Steve."

Coralynn caught her breath. Her first thought was that something bad had happened. Why else would Steve Markovich, their friend and owner of the Dalmatcia Hotel, call?

"What has happened?" she asked in a panic. "Is it my uncle or mother?"

Michael took her hand to calm her, saying, "It is nothing like that. Calm down." He patted her hand. "Steve called asking us if we could find the time to go to Gary and place flowers on Katya's grave."

Coralynn let out a long sigh of relief, saying, "Oh, Michael, I could only think it was bad news."

Michael said, "I hope you don't mind that I told him we would go to Gary tomorrow."

When she didn't reply, he went on. "He told me which train to take to Gary and what trolley to take to 14th Avenue and then how far to walk to a place called Milan's Tavern. There someone named Mato will give us directions to the cemetery."

Coralynn looked at Michael somewhat surprised, asking, "Are we going to get lost?"

Before Michael could reply, the man driving the cab said in his accented English, "Forgive me, but I couldn't help overhearing your conversation. I apologize, but maybe I can help."

Michael leaned forward in his seat to better hear the driver. "What do you mean?" he asked.

The driver, stopping at an intersection where a policeman was directing traffic, said, "I know the way to Gary and some parts of the city. On more than one occasion, I have driven steel mill executives from Chicago to the mills or the Gary Hotel."

Michael said, "That would be very nice, but I don't know how long we would be in Gary. Possibly more than a couple of hours and then we would still need to take the trains back to Chicago."

"I could spend the day." said the driver, driving on as the traffic started to move again. "I could pick you up at the hotel whenever you would be ready to leave."

Michael looked at Coralynn, who said nothing, and just returned his gaze.

The cab stopped at the Michigan Avenue entrance of the lovely Gold Coast hotel.

Michael helped Coralynn out of the cab before the driver could get out to the door. Michael put money in the man's hand, asking, "Can you be here at ten in the morning? That is, if you are still willing to spend the day in Gary."

Smiling, the short, curly-haired driver with bright eyes said, "Yes, Mr. DuKane, I will be here."

Both Michael and Coralynn looked at the driver in surprise. Michael asked, "How did you know my name?"

Smiling, and a bit embarrassed, the driver said, "Most of Chicago knows about you and your show. I turned down two fares hoping to get you to ride in my cab."

Michael, somewhat surprised at what the driver said, asked, "What is your name?"

"Antonio…Tony." He replied.

Michael shook Tony's hand saying, "Thank you, Tony. See you at ten in the morning."

At the lavish, crystal-chandeliered lobby of the Drake, Michael stopped at the desk for their room key and for any messages.

At the elevator, Michael asked Coralynn, "Are you ready for some early supper?"

Stepping into the carpeted elevator, Michael told the nicely dressed operator, wearing a blue and gold uniform, to take them to the sixth floor.

Once in their room, Coralynn went directly to the long panel windows facing Lake Michigan. She so enjoyed seeing the sun glowing on the sand and hearing the splash of the waves on Lake Michigan.

Still looking out the window, she said over her shoulder to Michael, "I would love to walk along the beach." She laughed, watching a man toss a ball and his dog running after it. "Did you hear me Michael? Can we walk on the beach?"

When Michael didn't answer, Coralynn turned to see him slumped in a soft lounging chair.

Concerned she hurried to him and knelt at his side, asking, "Michael, are you alright?"

Coralynn was more concerned when she saw the look on his face. "Oh, Michael," she asked, "what is wrong?"

In a low voice, Michael said, "What if the show is not a success? What if we leave Chicago in disgrace after all the money the store has spent on us?"

Coralynn sat back on her heels, staring at Michael. In all the years she had known him in New Orleans, she had only seen a confident man, a talented artist proud of his work.

She said, her voice low, "Michael...this is not like you. Why do you doubt your talent?"

"You heard Tony, the cab driver. He said I was the talk of Chicago. What if I don't live up to all that is expected of me?"

Coralynn stood up. She and Michael were living up to their arrangement and had not been intimate, as had been their agreement. Now, for the first time, she put her arms around his shoulders, hoping to comfort him. She said, "Michael, you are even a better artist than you think you are. Do you think all that is being done for the gallery show would be, if the people in charge did not think you were a great artist…and that they would not be getting a return on their investment?"

When Michael did not reply, Coralynn moved away. He looked up at her, asking, "Would you mind if we had supper here in the room. I don't feel like going to the dining room."

"Of course not." said Coralynn. "This is a beautiful room, with a beautiful view. It is all very elegant." As an afterthought she said, "I wonder if we could have some wine with our meal. You might sleep better."

After a meal of Lake Perch with apple pie for dessert, each had changed to their night clothes, Michael in a knee-length night shirt and Coralynn in a blue cotton long nightgown.

Both were in bathrobes. Again, Coralynn was looking at the lake. She said, "The city sounds of Chicago are so very different from New Orleans. It even smells different."

Michael, with his wine glass in hand, came and stood beside her. He looked out at the lake saying, "We will walk along the lake before we leave."

Coralynn said, "I am glad we are here." She turned and looked up at him saying, "I didn't think I would like it here in the North, but it hasn't been so bad, has it?"

Thoughtfully, Michael said, "It isn't over yet. Let's hope we don't go back to New Orleans in disgrace."

The room had two beds. Coralynn always slept in the one nearest the open window, so she could hear the waves, smell the lake, and hear the gulls in the morning. There were nights when she would get up and stare at the lake in the moonlight.

CHAPTER 3

Antonio...Tony, the cab driver, was in the parkway of the Drake Hotel waiting for Michael and Coralynn as arranged.

Tony smiled when he saw Michael, dressed in a collarless light blue shirt, again not tucked into his trousers. Today a large silver cross hung from his neck. The cab driver had never seen anyone who dressed as Michael DuKane did. Tony admired the artist for having a style of his own.

Coralynn was dressed as she had been the day before, in her ankle-length white dress with the pink cloth panels ending at her knees.

Tony took the turn to the Lake Shore road, which pleased Coralynn, who rolled down her cab window so that she could hear the splashing of the waves and see the clear blue water. Then he drove by the Chicago stock yards, known as Chicago's world-famous wonder. There were 475 acres of pens that held cattle, hogs, or sheep. It was here that many immigrants from Europe found work. Princes and maharajas and practically every tourist came to see the stock pens which stretched as far as the eye could see.

Both Coralynn and Michael had never seen anything like this. Where New Orleans smelled of flowers, this part of Chicago, the stockyards, had the overwhelming scent of the thousands of various livestock.

Michael was not as excited about the scenery during the drive to Gary or of Tony's descriptions as was Coralynn. He was still concerned that his show would not be a success.

He only half listened as Tony pointed to a field near a place called Whiting where Tony said, "A few years ago there was a Gypsy camp here. They have moved on. Maybe on their own, or were driven out."

Along the roadside, here and there, were food stands. Baskets of apples, pears, and occasionally blackberries were available to buy.

As the cab got closer to the city of Gary, one could see some lovely homes where the mill executives and prominent men of the city lived.

Coralynn looked at the homes with the well-manicured lawns, she said, "Gary looks like a beautiful city."

Tony paused before replying. "We are in the north part of the city. When you see the southern part, the part where the immigrant mill workers and the Blacks live, you may not be as impressed."

Before Coralynn could ask him more, he said, "Driving the mill executives from Chicago to Gary, I overhear many conversations. My father came to America to work, so when I hear what these rich mill owners say about the workers, I can almost hate them."

Now Tony had gotten Michael's attention. Michael leaned forward asking, "What do you mean, Tony?"

Slowing the car to a stop so that a group of people could cross the street, Tony said, "Two weeks ago I drove a couple men from the Blackstone Hotel to the main office building of the steel mill. These men were dressed in the finest light brown suits, shiny shoes, silk ties, and homburg hats."

He stopped speaking as he saw the last person cross the street. Shifting the car into gear, he continued the drive. He was silent for a while and just before Michael started to ask him to continue with his story, Tony said, "One of the men was talking about the workers. He said they were all lazy and costing the company money. He said they took too many breaks and weren't working fast enough." Now the tone of his voice changed to one bordering disgust. "These mill workers put in 12-hour shifts for 17 cents an hour. I have heard stories of men getting hurt on the job and if they can't work…well, too bad. They are left on their own to starve if they don't have any help."

Tony made a point of driving to 4th Avenue just in time to see some workers as they left the mill gates. Coralynn had never seen such sad, worn out looking men. Their trousers were black with oil or soot. Their shoes had burn holes on the tops from hot steel landing on them.

The sad and tired group of men walked slowly, carrying their metal bucket-shaped lunch pails.

As Tony drove on, he said, "Last year was bad for the mill workers. Many of them were laid off. I heard that their children dug through the garbage of the homes on the north side for anything they could eat."

This year is much better, with the war in Europe, more steel is shipped overseas.

On 5th and Broadway, Tony pointed to the beautiful Gary Hotel where many mill executives stayed when in town. On the street one could see nicely-dressed people going in and out of shops with beautifully-displayed merchandise in the windows. The electric streetcars were filled with riders.

Tony turned west to get to Washington Street. There was less auto traffic here. Coralynn could see several mill workers walking on this street. They walked the 15 or even 20 blocks to where they lived, so as not to spend the 5 cents for a ride on the streetcars. Many of the men walking stared at the unfamiliar sight of a yellow cab.

Both Michael and Coralynn could see the change in the look of the homes on the south side of Gary, compared to the lovely homes they saw as they came into Gary at the northern part of the city.

Coralynn stared at the almost makeshift houses. Some appeared to have been put together with found or discarded wood. Almost all the homes had some sort of fencing of either wood or wire. Gardens could be seen along with some chickens wandering loose in the yards.

People along the road stared at the cab, having never seen one in their neighborhood.

At their destination, men were standing in front of a one-story, narrow wooden building with the name MILAN'S boldly painted on the wall.

Tony pulled up close to the door, surprising the men standing in front of the building. Tony got out and asked, "Does anyone know Mato?"

"I get him for you." said one of the men in broken English, as he headed for the door. The other men stared at the cab while a couple went closer and looked through the window to see who was inside.

Seeing Michael with his long hair and beard, wearing a large cross, one of the men said, "Looks like a Serbian priest."

Coralynn felt uncomfortable seeing the men looking at them. Having seen the neighborhood they were in and the men in their work clothes, Coralynn said to Michael, "I can't believe this is where Steve lived. Look how poor this area is."

A man came hurrying out the door. The man that went in the building to find Mato pointed to Tony as the man asking for him."

Surprised to see the cab in front of his building and asking for him by name, Mato said, "I am Mato. What is wrong? What do you want?"

Tony opened the passenger door so that Michael could step out. Mato's eyes grew large seeing how this stranger was dressed.

Michael offered his hand to the confused Mato, saying "We are friends of Steve Markovich. He told me that you would show us where his wife's grave is. Steve wanted us to visit it for him.

After a long moment, while Mato grasped what Michael was saying, he asked, "Stevo? Stevo in New Orleans asked you to come see me?"

The crowd of on lookers was growing, with them whispering to one another, "Stevo, Stevo Markovich, he wants them to go to the cemetery."

Mato hesitated, not sure what to do. He was so very surprised and a little confused. He said, "I'll be right back. I go tell my Mrs. we go to cemetery."

Mato was a short man, slight of build. His hair was dark brown as were his eyes. As he hurried into the building, he pulled off his bar apron.

Michael was back in the cab when Mato returned in a couple minutes with a partially-empty wine bottle in his hand. Not only was his wife, Ivanka, with him, but when some of the tavern patrons heard that friends of Stevo's were outside in a yellow cab, they came along.

Tony held open the door to the front seat for Mato, which impressed the men watching. The small gathering of people watched in awe as Mato and the strangers drove off in the cab.

Mato said, "Keep straight on this road. The cemetery is not in Gary, but in Tolleston." Michael leaned forward tapping Mato on the shoulder. When Mato turned to face him, Michael extended his hand saying, "I am Michael." Nodding towards Coralynn, he said "And this is my wife, Coralynn. We are both close friends of Steve's. In fact, I am a small partner in his hotel."

Mato's voice was low and full of wonder when he asked, "Stevo owns a hotel?" Then he quickly asked, "Is it a nice hotel?"

Coralynn interrupted saying, "It is a wonderful hotel, one of the finest in New Orleans."

Mato, seated so that he was half turned, facing Michael asked, "Are you a priest?"

Coralynn couldn't keep from laughing, which embarrassed Mato.

Michael gave Coralynn a stern look, as if she had been a naughty child. He then said to Mato, "No, I am not a priest. I paint pictures and," he lifted his cross, "I wear big necklaces. Don't be embarrassed." said Michael, "I always dress this way and always wear jewelry."

Mato nodded, saying, "We miss Stevo. And…we miss Tomo. They were both so good to everyone. I know things were not the same for Stevo after Katya died."

"Here, turn here." said Mato, pointing to a curve in the road. "You can park along the grass there."

The cemetery was small and the land was level.

Mato and Michael each opened their own doors, while Tony was promptly out of the car opening the door for Coralynn.

Coralynn stared open mouthed at the cemetery. She asked in wonder, "Where are the crypts and the mausoleums? And what are all those stones sticking up out of the ground?"

Being from New Orleans where all graves are above ground, this cemetery was a surprise to her.

"Over here." said Mato, pointing to four graves. He led the way with the wine bottle still in his hand.

He stopped in front of an oval-shaped grave stone with the name Katya Markovich on it.

Coralynn and Michael stared at the stone, not sure what they should do. Coralynn said, "Oh Michael, we forgot to bring flowers."

Michael nodded saying, "Yes, we should have. Steve asked me to do so."

The four graves in a row were cared for, all having the same flowers planted next to the grave stones.

Tony stood back away from the three friends of Stevo's. He was a slight man with a light brown mustache matching his light brown hair. Being Italian and a Catholic, he bowed his head and said a silent prayer.

Michael had an odd feeling as he looked at Katya's gravestone. The spirit of Katya had come to him in a dream. It was that night that he immediately got out of bed and painted her portrait from the memory of his dream. So much had happened since the night he painted the portrait. It was what had been the beginning of his paintings of beautiful women. It is now why he was invited to have a show of his paintings in Fields.

Coralynn looked at the grave next to Katya's. The name on the stone was Julia Mandich. Coralynn knew that Tom's last name was Mandich, so she asked Mato, "Was this someone related to Tom, perhaps his sister?"

Mato kissed his fingertips and touched the grave stone saying, "No, this was Tomo's young bride."

Coralynn and Michael exchanged surprised looks. Never had Tom mentioned a wife.

Mato saw the exchanged looks and explained, "Julia died during her pregnancy. She didn't know what was wrong and died before the doctor was called."

A warm breeze grew stronger, picking up the faint scent of flowers in the cemetery. A grey bird settled on the top of Katya's stone.

Mato said, "Always a bird comes when we are here." He walked to the grave next to Julia's, saying. "Here is Ivan. He was Katya's first husband. They came from Europe together."

Again, Coralynn and Michael exchanged looks. They were learning facts about their friends that they had never heard.

Mato, once again kissed his fingertips, this time touching Ivan's stone, saying, "Ivan was killed by a motor car right in front of Stevo's store."

Mato came and stood in front of the stones of Katya and Milan. He sat down on the ground. Michael and Coralynn exchanged looks. Michael gave a nod and the two of them sat on the grass next to Mato.

A white rabbit peaked from behind Katya's stone, as if his space were being invaded.

Coralynn looked at Ivan's grave at one end and at Milan's next to Katya. She wondered why Katya was not next to Ivan.

Mato, stretching his legs out to be more comfortable, saw her look at the graves and read her mind. He said, "Stevo and Milan were great friends. Not only the best of friends..." here he paused, "but, both terribly in love with Katya."

Coralynn's eyes grew wide and her mouth dropped open. Before she could ask, "But, why?" regarding the close burial of Milan to Katya, Mato said, "Stevo knew how much it hurt Milan to lose Katya. So, he made it up to his friend by placing them side by side forever."

Coralynn's eyes glistened with tears. She looked at Michael, who also appeared touched by the story. Coralynn said to Michael, "Tom and Steve are our friends and we don't really know them."

Mato, still holding the wine bottle, said, "Whenever Stevo and Milan visited Katya here together, they would drink a bottle of wine. So whenever I come, I bring some wine." He pulled the cork from the bottle and poured what wine there was onto Milan's grave.

They were quiet on the drive back to the tavern thinking of what they had learned about their friends. Even Tony found the story of Katya and Milan spending eternity side by side touching.

There were a couple men outside of Milan's tavern watching for their return. One of the men hurried to the door shouting their arrival.

Mato's wife, Ivanka, her brown hair in a coiled braid around her head, hurried to the cab, as Mato opened his door to exit.

Ivanka pulled open the door on Michael's side and said, "Come, come. People want to meet Stevo's friends who come from far away." She reached in and pulled at his arm.

Michael looked confused. Before he could ask, Tony said, "I know these people. It is the same with Italians. They want to show us their hospitality. Go on in." He opened Coralynn's door for her and smiled at her look of confusion.

Tony got into the cab just as Mato came to his side of the car and said, "Park car in back, over there." he pointed. "You come in, sit with us, drink a little, eat a little."

Tony smiled as he drove his cab to the backyard of the tavern. This would be just like Italian hospitality, but instead of pasta, it would be sausages and garlic.

As soon as Michael and Coralynn entered the smoke-filled room, they were accosted by almost everyone in the tavern. All of them wanted to shake hands with the friends of Stevo Markovich, not knowing they were already in Chicago, but some thinking they were sent from New Orleans just to visit the graves.

Awed by Michael's way of dressing, many believed him to be a priest, probably Orthodox.

Mato shooed the people away as Ivanka had a table ready for them. It was not common for a table in Milan's to have a cloth on it, but this one did along with a couple of lilac sprigs in a glass of water, probably taken from someone's yard.

At the far wall some tamburashi…musicians, started to play on their stringed prims and braches.

To Michael's dismay, Ivanka came to the table with a tray holding two shot glasses of slivovitza, the popular Croatian plum brandy. He moaned under his breath, "Oh, God."

Coralynn was looking at all the people and listening to the music. When she heard Michael moan she asked concerned, "What is it?"

Smiling at the people watching them, he said softly, "I hate this drink. When I am Tomo's Little Zagreb, I can't stand the smell of it."

"Michael," said Coralynn being very serious, "You have to drink this."

He whispered, "And then throw up?"

Almost everyone in the room had a drink, slivovitza or pivo...beer.

Coralynn leaned her head close to Michael's, whispering, "Let's entwine our wrists and put our heads close together appearing to drink. I will drink mine and slip the empty glass into your hand while you slip your full glass to me."

"Then what?" he whispered back at her.

She hissed, "Just DO IT!"

Tony was sitting at the bar watching the crowd as they shouted the familiar toast, Nazdravljie...to health.

Coralynn, who had been brought up to be a proper Southern lady, tossed down her glass of plum brandy like a Croatian peasant. With the dexterity of a magician, she switched the empty glass for the full one, which she also tossed down. It was followed with a slight shiver and a warm sensation she had never felt before.

Everyone in the bar cheered and applauded that their guests had joined them with a shot of slivovitza.

Coralynn and Michael smiled at the crowd which was dispersing as the dance music started.

Michael looked at Coralynn's flushed face, asking, "Are you alright?"

"Whew," she said a bit breathless. "I didn't know what to expect, but it wasn't bad." She smiled, "In fact, it was rather pleasant."

Michael occasionally had eaten at Tomo's Little Zagreb and was familiar with sarma...stuffed cabbage rolls, palacinke... cheese crepes, and even a Croatian favorite, their barbequed lambs. But, he was not ready for kishka...blood sausage, grah I zele...sauerkraut and beans, or for a plate full of chopped onions and cevaps...tiny fried sausages of ground meat.

Coralynn and Michael's appearance, because of Stevo, had become an honored event with food for everyone in the tavern.

Ivanka hovered over them, thrilled to have them in the tavern. People would be talking about this for a month or more, often with exaggerations to make their stories better.

Michael, having grown up in France and living for so long in New Orleans, was not familiar with the food put before them.

Tony, at the bar, felt right at home. Growing up in an immigrant neighborhood, he, like others, had learned different customs and often some different languages. He dove right into the onions and cevaps.

Michael tried to hide his look of shock as Coralynn immediately started on the onions and cevaps. Not stopping there, she cut and tasted the blood sausage.

To be polite, Michael did eat some of the sauerkraut and beans, finding them not as bad as he had expected.

"Yedi,Yedi...eat, eat." urged Ivanka. "I got kolachki in kitchen."

When Ivanka placed a plate of prune and cheese pastries on the table, Michael's mood brightened.

It wasn't long before the kolo...circle dancing, started. Men outnumbered the women in the tavern, but that made no difference, as men doing circle dancing was common in most European countries.

Coralynn was tapping her hand in time to the music. She watched the dance steps, two to the right, step forward, two to the left, step backward and move on in the circle. Coralynn stood up. "Let's dance." She announced.

"Are you crazy?" asked Michael. "My stomach is still trying to behave after all those beans and sauerkraut."

She shrugged her shoulders, dismissing Michaels's complaint. She went to the dance floor. There were cheers when the fancy lady, in her long white and pink dress, joined in the kolo dancing. Different men cut into the dance just to be able to hold Coralynn's hand for a while, before someone else broke into the circle.

Coralynn laughed and had a wonderful time dancing. She was a different person here. So very different from the Coralynn of New Orleans where she had to be so careful of her behavior, knowing that her reputation was already tarnished because her father had been a thief.

The music changed to a couples dance.

Tony left his seat at the bar and came to sit with Michael. He nodded towards the dance floor, where a line of men were waiting to dance with Coralynn. A man would tap her dance partner on the shoulder to cut in.

Tony asked Michael, "Why aren't you dancing with your wife?"

Michael answered seriously, "I think I would be spoiling her fun. I have never seen her enjoy herself so much. This is a different woman from the one I married in New Orleans."

At last, Coralynn smiled at the men and shook her head, meaning, no more. Her face was flushed from dancing and perspiration glistened on her face and neck.

While Coralynn was fanning her face with a napkin, Michael asked Tony, "Do you think Mato would give me some of that white butcher paper I see behind the food table?" As Tony got up, Michael added, "Two pieces." He held up his hands to show the size he wanted.

Tony returned shortly with the two pieces of paper that Michael requested.

Coralynn said, "Michael, I think I need to go out for some air. It is so hot in here."

Absent mindedly spreading the paper on the table, Michael said, "You go ahead. Go out and cool off."

Coralynn stood up, staring at Michael, who now had a pencil in his hand that he had fished out of his pocket.

She shook her head, saying to Tony, "Now he wants to draw!"

"Come on," said Tony, "let's go out by the cab, it is in back in the shade."

There was an animal pen far back of the tavern beyond the house. In it were two lambs and a goat. The goat was probably for milk with which to make cheese.

Tony said to Coralynn, "I know I said we could stay all day, but we have been here a long time."

She agreed, "We have been here much longer than I thought we would be."

Tony offered Coralynn a cigarette, which she declined, saying, "When you finish the cigarette, I will remind Michael that it is time to leave."

Coralynn went into the tavern alone, while Tony moved the car back to the tavern entrance.

There were some people around Michael, watching him as he sketched one picture of Ivanka and was just finishing the one of Mato. There were murmurs of approval and men nudging one another to look at Michael while he sketched.

When the sketching was finished, a man called out to Mato & Ivanka.

"A yoy, kako ljepo…Oh, my how pretty. Hvala…thank you." said Ivanka overwhelmed by such a wonderful gift. "Gleday…look." she said to Mato, who also was so very pleased.

He shook Michael's hand, "Hvala, mnogo hvala…Thank you, many thanks."

Coralynn sat next to Michael. "I think we should be leaving."

"Yes." He agreed. "I didn't think we would be here so long." Then he added, "We couldn't walk out on these wonderful people. I am glad we stayed. They have been so very nice to us."

Ivanka came to the table with shot glasses and more slivovitza. When everyone had a drink in their hand, Mato, his arm around Ivanka, made a toast.

"To our new friends, who came to us from our old friend, Stevo, ZIVILI…to life."

Coralynn drank her slivovitza in one swallow. She quickly switched glasses with Michael and downed his unwanted drink.

Everyone followed Michael and Coralynn out to the cab to say farewell. Some of the men went to the driver's side of the car and shook hands with Tony wishing him a good trip to Chicago.

Never in her life had Coralynn been kissed by so many people, had her hand either kissed or shook as she did in front of this tavern in a "not-so-nice" section of Gary, Indiana.

A bit tired and overwhelmed by the day, the three were quiet as Tony found his way to route 20 leading out of Gary.

They had been driving for about half an hour in silence. Coralynn leaned her head on Michael's shoulder. It surprised him. He was more surprised when she put her hand on his knee and he felt her hand slowly moving upward.

Stunned he said, "Coralynn...Coralynn? Do you know what you are doing?"

She replied in a soft voice, "Won't the hotel maid be surprised when she has only one bed to make up tomorrow!"

CHAPTER 4

In the second story of their rented Lincoln Park home, Stefan Vladeslav was moving about as quietly as if he were a burglar or a man sneaking out for a rendezvous.

On this Sunday morning, he didn't want to awaken his wife and explain where he was going.

Once outside, dressed in his brown gabardine suit, silk tan tie, brown boot type shoe, and his homburg hat, he hurried down the block to the corner where he found a cab. He instructed the driver to take him to Morse and Paulina Streets where a little wooden Catholic Church had been built in 1912.

Stefan was drawn to this church because it was Croatian and Catholic.

The church was crowded and Mass had started. Removing his hat, Stefan found a place in a pew on the side. He slid into place and knelt, making the sign of the cross. He was filled with emotion. He never thought he would miss his homeland or his religion as much as he was experiencing now. Back home in the Croatian part of his father's land, Vladezemla, there had been a chapel in back of the house, where more than once he sat and prayed.

Stefan was aware that the people around him were openly staring at him. He was dressed so elegantly compared to the simple people who lived in this neighborhood and who worked at any job they could find. Everyone was clean and dressed in their best simple clothing. Many of the women still wore what they did back in the old country, long skirts and long-sleeved blouses, most with some sort of red embroidered designs.

Ignoring the looks and stares of those near him, Stefan was deep in thought. He had come to church for a sign of some sort as to what to do with his life.

He watched as children and many adults went to the altar to receive communion. It had been years since he had communion. He had done so many wrong things in the past few years that he could not think of taking communion.

Stefan was so lost in his thoughts, that he barely noticed the Mass was over. He stepped aside and let people file out of the pew. He sat down and looked at the altar with the brass candlesticks. Two altar boys came out of the vestibule and snuffed out the candles, glancing over at Stefan as he sat alone in the now empty church.

He glanced at the paintings of saints. He studied the crosses and the hanging incense burner near the altar. There was a statue of Mother Mary or Velka Gospa, as she was known to the parishioners of St. Jerome's. Some lit candles flickered beneath her feet. These lit candles were petitions for something wanted or for the soul of someone gone.

Stefan was so lost in thought, that he had not noticed someone standing near him. He was startled when he became aware of a gentle-faced, smiling Friar looking at him.

No longer in his church vestments, but back in his simple brown robes, the smiling priest asked, "Are you alright? May I sit next to you?"

Stefan was unsure of what to say and a little embarrassed. He said, "I am not a member of this church."

The friar had a round, cherubic face. He had a thin body and was not very tall. He said, "That doesn't matter. You must be here for a reason." Then, pointing to the empty place next to Stefan, he asked, "May I join you?"

Stefan moved over, making more room for the friar, who introduced himself, "I am Stipe Loncar from Hercegovina."

Stefan offered his hand saying, "I am Stefan Vladeslav from outside of Zagreb."

Father Loncar said, "Well, Stefan, I can see you are troubled. Is it anything I might help you with?"

When Stefan did not answer immediately, Father Loncar said, "Let's go to my room at the side of the church where we can talk more privately." He said this noticing a man and woman had come into the church to light candles. Both men exited the pew, genuflecting as they made the sign of the cross.

This was not like Stefan to even think about talking about his problems with someone he had just met, even a priest. But then, he remembered Father Lahdra, back home, and what a trusted friend the priest was to his family in Vladezemla.

Father Loncar lived in a simple, one-room dwelling very near the side of the church. It was a wooden structure, as was the church.

Stefan was offered a chair at a round, wooden table while Father Loncar busied himself getting glasses and a bottle of wine. The room reflected the simple life of the Friar, clean, tidy, but sparse.

Father Loncar did not ask Stefan if he wanted any wine, as he filled the simple drinking glass. He then filled his own before sitting down across from Stefan.

He lifted his glass in a toast to Stefan saying, "Nazdravljie."

Stefan returned the toast and took a sip of the blessed holy wine.

Loncar's brown eyes looked deep into Stefan's blue eyes. He said, "Now, what brought you to St. Jerome's and to me. God sent you to me for a reason."

Stefan blinked several times. He thought to himself, *Am I supposed to talk to this priest? Can I tell him everything? Is that why I am here?*

Father Loncar said, "There is nothing you can tell me that will shock me. In the confessional I can't think of anything I have not heard."

Seeing an ashtray on the table, Stefan asked, "May I smoke?"

Father Loncar nodded yes. When Stefan offered him a cigarette from his gold case Father Loncar declined.

Stefan took a sip of wine and lit his cigarette. Father Loncar waited patiently for Stefan to speak.

After a bit, Stefan said, "I left my wife in Zagreb. She kept returning to Germany to look after her father and it angered me when she was gone for long periods."

Father Loncar said nothing, just listened.

"There was more," said Stefan. "I was not kind to her when she lost my sons during two different pregnancies."

Still, the priest said nothing, but Stefan thought he detected some slight change in those brown eyes.

Stefan stood up and started pacing. He said, "We had a business to run and Barbra was the only one who knew how to do the pricing and the buying. Without her it was failing."

Before Father Loncar could ask about the business, Stefan said, "I inherited the building with all the antiques in it. Barbra knew about such things, while I knew nothing."

Stefan paced the length of the small room. He was silent for a while. He said in a low and shameful voice, "I let my pride take over. I couldn't let myself admit that she was the reason the business had been a success."

He stopped his pacing, picked up the wine glass and took a long drink. Looking at Father Loncar, who still showed no reaction to what Stefan had said, he continued. "I bought tickets for America. I had some of our paintings packed for shipping. I became angrier with each day when I did not hear from her. I wasn't going to wait any longer. It was obvious her father was more important to her than I was." Stefan took a deep breath. He stubbed out his cigarette and said, "I brought our servant to America in Barbra's place."

Father Loncar asked, "What is it you want from me? Advice? Or do you want my forgiveness?"

Stefan sat down and took another cigarette from his case. After he lit it, he said, "I just needed someone to talk to. I have no friends I can tell any of this to."

He blew a puff of smoke into the air, "You see, Father, I married an American woman, a Presbyterian."

Now he got a surprised reaction from Father Loncar, who said, "But you already had a wife."

Stefan explained, "I didn't like the people I was staying with. I didn't know them. I thought when I came to America that I would stay with my cousin, but she had died." He waived his hand in the air as he continued with his explanation.

"I met Adele in a fancy hotel. She was beautiful and a wealthy widow. I knew she would give me the kind of life I wanted in America."

"And, did she?" ask Father Loncar.

"Yes." said Stefan. "Yes, at first I loved our life together. She knew all the wealthy men who were connected with the steel mill in Gary. And, she was the widow of a man from a banking family in Cleveland."

Now he sat down, sitting across from Father Loncar, his voice low and serious, "It was the way these men who owned the steel mill talked about our people...I bit my tongue wanting to defend them."

He saw the questioning look in Loncar's eyes. He said, "These men from the Old Country work long, hard, terrible hours and are called lazy. I saw these men and I felt guilty sitting the lobby of the Gary Hotel, watching them stagger home to the poor section of Gary.

Father Loncar said, "I sense you want to do something, but you haven't told me what it is."

A small smile played on Stefan's lips. He said, "I want to leave my American wife."

Loncar looked at him, tilting his head, a questioning look in his eyes.

Stefan said, "I know where my wife Barbra is." Before Father Loncar could say anything, Stefan continued, "I was in Marshall Fields just walking around when I saw some paintings." Stefan's eyes glistened with a bit of excitement. He said with almost a tone of astonishment, "There was a painting of Barbra for sale." He went on excitedly, "I spoke with the artist and he knows Barbra and told me she lives in New Orleans. I even know the street where she lives."

"Did you tell him who you were?" asked Father Loncar, concern showing in his eyes.

"No." said Stefan, "Not even when I bought the painting."

Father Loncar asked, shooing away a persistent fly, "What did your wife think of the painting?"

"She doesn't know." said Stefan. "I have it hidden under my bed."

Father Loncar stood up, going to the window to close it. The flies could smell the wine. He leaned his back against the closed window. After a moment he said, "So Stefan. You have unburdened yourself. You want me to tell you what to do, but I can't. It is your life."

Stefan smiled, saying, "I know what I am going to do. Now, after saying my thoughts out loud, I know that I am going to New Orleans to find Barbra."

CHAPTER 5

It was about two in the afternoon when Stefan got out of the cab in front of the house in Lincoln Park. He saw the window curtain move and he knew that Adele had been watching for him.

He found the front door of the house unlocked. When he opened it, he saw a very beautiful and a very angry Adele. Her pink lips were pursed together, while her dark eyes glared at him.

"How dare you!" she shouted. "How dare you leave and not let me know where you are going. Couldn't you leave a note...better still, could you not have awakened me?"

Stefan hung his hat on a brass hook in the entryway. He was very calm as he smiled at Adele, saying, "I went to church."

"You couldn't wait for me?" she practically screamed at him.

In a very calm tone of voice, he said, "I went to a Catholic church."

Adele, dressed in a blue lace dress had her hands on her hips. She couldn't believe her ears. Again she shouted at him, "You went to church with those bead rattlers."

Again in a calm voice, Stefan said, "I was raised in the Catholic faith. There are times I find it comforting."

Stefan walked towards the kitchen. He was hungry. He had not eaten since the night before.

A very annoyed Adele followed him, shouting, "Stay here and talk to me."

Still in a calm speaking voice, Stefan said, "I am hungry." He poured himself a cup of coffee with an equal amount of milk, European style.

Adele, still angry, watched as he opened the two-door wooden icebox. She said, "Church does not last till two in the afternoon."

Stefan ignored her remark, as he took a plate of ham out of the icebox, along with a small, cold potato. Finding a knife in a drawer, he sat at the table and cut off a slice of ham. He ate it with his fingers.

Adele, now more worried than angry, looked long at her very calm husband. She sat in the chair facing him. She watched him as he bit into the potato, waiting for him to say something. In a very low, calm voice, she asked, "What could be troubling you so much that you needed a priest?

Couldn't you talk to me?"

When he didn't answer, she felt a cold chill. In their two years of marriage he had always been so very polite, so attentive. Now…now he seemed, well…remote. Deep inside of her, there was a feeling she never had before. It was fear. It was as if the Stefan sitting across from her, calmly eating ham, was someone she did not know.

There was a knock at the door. Adele jumped, startled by the sound. She was so involved with Stefan that she forgot her good friend from Gary, Grace Adams, had sent a car for her.

She rose from her chair, not wanting to leave to go to the door, but knew she had to.

Adele was back in minutes. She put her hand on Stefan's shoulder. He didn't look up. Her heart felt cold. She said, "I have to meet Grace. I am helping her with the invitations for the charity ball next month."

When Stefan didn't answer, she continued, "We are having dinner at the Hofbrauhaus in the city. Reservations are for 6:30."

Adele hesitated…bent to kiss him on the cheek. He didn't respond, just sipped his coffee. In a somewhat shaky voice, she said, "Remember to wear your evening clothes." She stood waiting for him to respond. When he said nothing, she left the room, going out to the waiting car.

In the car during the drive to the La Salle Hotel, Adele's mind was swirling with thoughts of her life with Stefan. She had been so very proud when she and Stefan married. Adele was the envy of all her friends for she had a very handsome European count, whose manners were so perfect that women who met him would openly criticize their own husbands for not behaving as Stefan did.

As Adele looked out of the cab window, she really didn't see anything. Her mind was so focused on Stefan. Today had been the first day that he did anything to distress her. She wondered why she had reacted so harshly. He had always been perfect in the past, never showing annoyance to anything she did or said.

She remembered the times she ranted about the fact that they had never been invited to any event hosted by the Austria-Hungarian consulate. It had infuriated her when he calmly said, it didn't matter. She had envisioned his home in Vladezemla to be a stone castle. Stefan never told her it was a very nice house, but not an estate. He also failed to tell her that he had in fact grown up playing with the children of the peasants on the farm lands.

Today was different. That is what disturbed Adele. Stefan, for the first time, appeared indifferent to her. In the past, if she showed worry or distress, he was so sympathetic, so very caring. Today he had been a stranger.

In the kitchen, Stefan put the ham in the brass-trimmed icebox. He left the soiled dishes and his coffee cup on the table.

Passing through the living room on the way upstairs, he spotted the September issue of the *Saturday Evening Post* magazine. He liked the magazine. Under the title of the magazine were the words, *An Illustrated Weekly Founded in 1728 by Benj. Franklin.* The cover depicted a young girl in a white dress carrying a red umbrella while holding a doll. The cover artist was Stella Weber.

Upstairs, Stefan went to his room, which adjoined Adele's. In his room was a door which gave access to Adele's very feminine bedroom.

Stefan's room was all in maroon and gray furnishings. A tall walnut, oval-mirrored chiffarobe, which was a cabinet meant to be half closet and half dresser, with drawers on one side, stood beautifully on a nearby wall.

He left his room going to a far door at the end of the hallway. He opened the door leading to the small attic-like storage area. He stepped in and pulled on the handle of a metal and wooden travel trunk.

Stefan manhandled the trunk, dragging it into his room. He undid the metal clasps to open the trunk. It did not lie on the floor, but stood up on the short end. It was actually a traveling closet. On one side was a bar with cloth-covered wire hangers for hanging clothing. On the other side were three drawers, the bottom one for shoes.

He didn't realize that he was smiling as he packed his shirts and ties. No longer would he have to listen to Adele and her wealthy friends make fun of the immigrants who he felt himself a strong part of. He had no trouble understanding the Italians or Greeks, even the Turks when they spoke their broken English.

More than once, Adele would look down with disdain at the Polish cleaning woman who took care of the house they were renting, often calling the woman dumb.

With the packing completed, Stefan knelt down and reached under his bed, pulling out the brown paper-wrapped parcel, which held the DuKane portrait of Barbra.

He held the wrapped package away from him, as if he were looking at the painting itself. Stefan sighed deeply. He felt he was going to start his life over again. This time it would be right.

Back at the chiffarobe, he lifted a loose board finding his briefcase. He didn't have to look in it. He knew that his bonds, his shares in the Gary Steel Mill and his stock in the Cleveland Bank were all there. Adele and her friends had been very generous to Stefan with their advice and help during his two year marriage to her.

Even before he had made the decision to go to New Orleans, some unknown force directed him to have his money from the Chicago City bank transferred to the New Orleans National Bank. Adele did not know that Stefan had his own bank account, as they had a joint account at the Chicago National Bank.

Stefan looked around the room to see if he had forgotten anything. He saw the custom made silver frame Adele had given him with their wedding picture in it. He wanted the frame. At the top of the frame was the Vladeslav family crest, while at the bottom was the Croatian Crest, the one depicted on the tiled roof of the Croatian Church in Zagreb.

He removed the picture from the frame. He re-opened the trunk and placed the empty frame in the drawer with his socks and underwear.

The door between the two rooms was open. As he walked through to Adele's mirrored dressing table, he slipped off his wedding ring. On the center of the dressing table he placed the wedding picture and on it he left his gold wedding ring.

The small metal ball wheels on the trunk were not useful on the stairs, so Stefan laid the trunk on its side and slid it down the carpeted staircase. Seeing the *Saturday Evening Post* magazine, he picked it up, folded it in half and slipped it into his suit pocket.

He went back upstairs for his briefcase and the wrapped painting. He took one last look at the life he was leaving.

He felt no regrets.

Standing outside of the house he watched for a cab. It didn't take long for an empty one to come by. Stefan waived and it moved to the curb.

At the Drake Hotel, Michael DuKane and his wife Coralynn, even in the mid-afternoon, were till in their bathrobes. Soiled dishes from their lunch were on a cart waiting to be removed.

Scattered on the floor were the Sunday newspapers. Coralynn was very excited as she read the praise in the papers of Michael's show at Fields. Also, there was a full-page ad showing photos taken by the photographer, Edda.

Coralynn practically squealed saying, "Michael we must get more newspapers. I want to send copies to everyone we know in New Orleans." Then she jumped up saying, "I will send one to the newspaper back home. I know they will print a story about your success here in Chicago."

When Michael did not reply, Coralynn asked, "What is the matter? You aren't listening to me."

He said, his voice thoughtful, "Do you remember the time we found out that Barbra was a Countess?"

She replied, "I didn't think anything of it. I thought it was a story or a joke."

Michael, seated in a soft chair, had business cards scattered on his lap.

Again, in a thoughtful tone, he said, "A very handsome and very well-dressed man came to the gallery. Michael studied the paintings shown in the newspaper. When he saw the one of Barbra, he looked faint."

Michael was flipping one of the business cards in the palm of his hand. He continued, "The man wanted to know all about Barbra. How it was that I painted her...even where she lived."

Now Michael stood up and slowly paced the floor. He looked at Coralynn. "I don't think I am exaggerating when I say he appeared pale and even a little unsteady on his feet. I offered him a chair. He wanted the painting right then. I watched him as he leaned on his walking stick waiting for the painting to be wrapped, which he insisted on taking with him right then."

Michael handed the embossed business card to Coralynn. The name on the card was COUNT STEFAN VLADISLAV.

CHAPTER 6

Stefan rode the Continental Limited train to Buffalo, New York. There he switched to the 20th Century Limited to New Orleans. It was advertised as the most famous train in the world.

Some Pullman cars had a form of privacy with two long seats across from one another. Two dark panels from floor to ceiling could be pulled together for privacy. It was such a place that Stefan wanted. He purchased all the seating for the small compartment. He insisted that his trunk be put on one of the seats. During the entire trip to New Orleans, Stefan stayed in his private area. He left his enclosed area only to use the men's washroom at the back of the car and to stretch his legs. He had the porter bring food to him along with any newspapers he could find.

The porter, dressed in his white coat, found some older issues of the English newspaper, *The Daily Mirror*. All of the headlines and articles had to do with the war. A mention was made that Germans dropped bombs from their zeppelins and another mentions the loss of a zeppelin in a raid.

Stefan wasn't interested in the war, though he wondered if it would not spread through Europe, perhaps into Yugoslavia.

In an American newspaper, he read that President Wilson claims to hold the peace. In the *Christian Science Monitor*, he read about the problems between China and Japan. *The New York Times* wrote that Ann Case, American soprano, will be heard again this season at the Metropolitan Opera House.

In another newspaper, he read about a young ball player named Babe Ruth. In 1914, Babe Ruth was signed to play minor league baseball for the Baltimore Orioles, but in 1915 he was sold to the Red Sox.

Stefan was getting bored with reading. He did occasionally leave his enclosed area and take a short walk up and down the aisle to stretch his legs.

This particular night he made sure the cloth panels were pulled shut. He checked to see that his briefcase was under his pillow. His wardrobe trunk was on its side on the other double seat. Taking off his shoes and suit jacket, he stretched out on the double seat to sleep. In the morning, he would be in New Orleans.

In Chicago, in the Marshall Fields Art Gallery, Michael DuKane was greeting and speaking with the many viewers of his paintings. When there was a lull in the visitors, Michael went into Mr. White's office.

Mr. White looked up at Michael, pleased to see Michael in a pale green Chinese full length shirt with a large Jade pendant hanging from his throat.

He asked, "What can I do for you, Michael? Need a break from talking to people?"

Michael smiled at the man who had made such a change in Michael's life.

He said, "No. But, I would like to make a call to New Orleans. I will be happy to pay for it."

Mr. White said, "If it is important to you, of course you may make the call. Just let me call the switchboard to approve it for you."

After speaking with the store's switchboard operator, Mr. White, always impeccably dressed, handed the phone to Michael, saying "Don't worry about the cost of the call."

A surprised Michael smiled as Mr. White left the office so that Michael could make his call in privacy.

After giving the switchboard operator the number and waiting for the many connections to be made before it reached New Orleans, he heard, "We have your call to New Orleans."

Michael heard several clicks and then Stevo Markovich's voice saying, "Hello...Hello."

"Hello, Steve. It is Michael. I am calling you from Chicago."

There was a surprised pause, then Stevo said, "Is anything wrong? Are you alright?"

Michael sat in the desk chair as he said, "Everything is fine here. We went to Gary to the cemetery."

There was a catch in Stevo's throat as he said, "Thank you, Michael. That means a lot to me." After a pause he added, "I hated leaving Katya alone."

Michael said in a comforting tone, "She isn't alone. She has Ivan and Milan with her.

"Ah," said Stevo. "That means Mato told you."

"Steve, your friends couldn't have been nicer to us. They fed us and treated us like family." said Michael.

"How is Coralynn?" asked Stevo. "Can she stand it up North?"

Michael let out a short laugh, saying, "She is a different person up here. She is not the Coralynn that left New Orleans." He laughed again. "In Gary at Milan's tavern, she drank slivovitza, danced the kolo, and then danced with strangers until she got tired."

Stevo asked, "How is your show going? Are you selling paintings?"

There was a long pause before Michael said, "Steve, that's the reason for this call."

When Stevo did not reply, Michael asked, "Do you know anyone named Stefan Vladeslav?"

There was no answer. Michael thought the phone connection had been lost. He asked, "Steve? Steve, are you there?"

Stevo's voice sounded different as if his vocal chords had tightened. Stevo asked, "Where did you hear that name?"

Michael insisted in a calm voice, "You haven't answered me. Do you know a Stefan Vladeslav?"

After another long pause before Stevo said, "He was Katya's cousin. He didn't know she had died when he and Ignatz came to America."

Michael's brain almost spun when he heard the words, *he and Ignatz came to America.*

Michael, almost in a daze, spoke slowly. "You mean to tell me that Ignatz knows this man?"

Stevo asked, now his voice stronger and almost demanding. "Tell me Michael, why are you asking about this Stefan?"

"Please, Steve." said Michael, "Tell me what you know about him."

Stevo answered cautiously, "I will tell you, only if you promise to tell me what you know about him and the reason for this phone call."

"I promise, Steve." said Michael as an uneasy feeling crept over him.

Stevo said, "To make a long story short, Stefan abandoned Barbra and came to America with Ignatz."

Michael almost stopped breathing when he heard this. Stevo continued, "After staying with me for a while, he started going about the city of Gary on his own. He was not pleased with the arrangements, having expected more elegance than my store and living quarters provided." When Michael said nothing, Stevo asked, "Are you still there, Michael?

"Yes, I am listening."

Stevo continued, "It wasn't long before Barbra and Josef came to Gary looking to join Stefan. I still remember the rainy and windy day in front of the Gary Hotel where I went to pick up Barbra and Josef. Stefan was with an American woman, who I knew well. Seeing Barbra he looked right through her as if she was not there."

Michael could hear Stevo strike a match to light a cigarette. He waited until Stevo started to speak again, "Stefan never returned to my place nor did he send word for Ignatz to join him. Now Barbra and Josef were staying with me. It was shortly after this that Barbra found out Stefan married the woman he was seen with."

Michael said nothing for a moment. Then Stevo heard him say in a very low voice, "Oh, shit."

"Michael…Michael, what is it?" Stevo felt a cold chill go through him, as if something bad was going to happen.

Michael said, in a very troubled voice, "Steve…Stefan Vladeslav was here in Marshall Fields for my art show. He…he stood in front of Barbra's portrait with a stunned look on his face. I thought he might faint. He bought the painting right then and insisted on taking it with him."

Michael felt very uneasy. He said, "Steve, he asked me about Barbra. I told him she was in New Orleans and I even told him she lives on Canal Street."

CHAPTER 7

The New Orleans Union Station was designed by Louis Sullivan. It was a large brick building with several arched entrances and exits.

Off the train and in the disembarking area, Stefan took a deep breath of the warm floral-scented air. The sun felt good on his face after spending a little more than two days in his draped space on the train.

There were horse-driven carriages which Stefan thought to be too small for the wardrobe trunk he had. He flagged down a vehicle that had an open ended back, almost like a truck. This was for luggage and packages.

"Welcome to New Orleans." said the driver, as he easily lifted the trunk on the back of the vehicle. "Where to?" he asked.

Seated comfortably in the back seat, Stefan said, "I don't know. This is my first trip here. Suggest a nice hotel to me."

The driver said, "There's the Royal Orleans, the Hotel Chalmette, and the Dalmatcia."

Hearing the name Dalmatcia, Stefan said, "The Dalmatcia." He decided that it had to be owned by a Croatian if it was call the Dalmatcia.

Stefan, like all new comers to New Orleans, was assaulted by the scent of flowers, the smell of the sea, and most of all, by the colorful mix of races that made up the charming city. He could hear the clanging of streetcars, the clip-clop of horse's hooves, along with the musical sounds of street musicians and the sing-song of women with baskets on their heads selling fruit or cakes.

As the auto neared the Dalmatcia Hotel, Stefan saw horse-drawn carriages belonging to the Dalmatcia, with drivers in red long coats and red top hats. Just before the driver pulled into the entrance of the hotel, Stefan saw a two-story building across the street with a wrought iron balcony on the second floor. Stefan smiled when he saw the sign on the front of the building, LITTLE ZAGREB. His own store in Europe had been in Zagreb.

Away from the hotel entrance, but nearby, some young Black boys were playing music on instruments made of buckets and boxes. Passersby tossed coins to the appreciative musicians.

A doorman, also dressed in the long red coat and red top hat, opened the door for Stefan. A porter came promptly to take Stefan's trunk.

Stefan looked about the lounge area of the hotel approvingly. He passed by Michael DuKane's glass-fronted studio, stopping to recognize the artists work.

At the front desk, he saw and admired the large painting on the back wall of Miss Kara, who had been Stevo's first friend in New Orleans and the common law wife of the local bank president. Stefan easily recognized Michael's painting style.

The day clerk at the desk was a young very nicely-dressed man. He wore a red flower on the lapel of his grey suitcoat.

"Welcome to the Dalmatcia." he said smiling warmly at Stefan. "Are you looking for a single or double room?" he asked.

Stefan said, "A single room." He glanced around the area, seeing the partial outdoor restaurant to the right and to the left, the hallway leading to the kitchen and some rooms which were for hotel personnel. In the rooms to the left were Stevo's office, Ignatz's room, and the other two, for now, storage.

Coming out of his office, a surprised Stevo saw Stefan signing the guest book. Stevo paused, almost going back into his office, but realized that sooner or later, he would have to see and speak with Stefan.

At the desk, Stevo handed a small leather case with the payroll for the employees to the man working the desk. He said, "Here, Louis, pass these out before you leave."

Stefan looked surprised to recognize Stevo standing almost next to him. He never expected to see Stevo. He had assumed Stevo was still in Gary.

He said, "Well, Stevo. So you are working here."

Before Stevo could reply, Louis said, "The hardest worker in the hotel."

Stefan smiled, saying, "Glad to see you have a job here."

Louis was surprised by this remark, but when Stevo didn't say anything, the desk clerk remained silent as he handed the room key to the porter.

The porter stood waiting for Stefan to follow him. Stevo didn't say anything more to Stefan, who stood there, somewhat undecided as to what more to say. As he turned to follow the porter to his room, he said to Stevo, "Well, since you work here, I suppose I will be seeing more of you."

There was no smile on Stevo's lips as he said, "Yes, I suppose you will be seeing more of me."

Louis, who didn't say anything, could feel the tension when he heard Stevo say, "I suppose you will be seeing more of me."

When Stefan was gone, Stevo said to Louis "If I am needed, I will be across the street at Little Zagreb."

Stevo smiled at the people he passed who were sitting in the comfortable chairs in the lounge. He practically ran out the door and across the street. The restaurant was not open for business as it was not yet noon, but the door was unlocked.

Ignatz was in the open kitchen area seeing that everything was in order. The small man, who loved both Stevo and Tomo like family, was pleased to see Stevo. Dobar Dan…Good Day, he greeted Stevo, who only nodded and asked, "Where is Tom?"

"Upstairs. He hasn't come down yet." said Ignatz.

Stevo, who had a fatherly relationship with Tomo, went to the curved metal stairs leading to the upper floor. He called out, "Tomo...Tomo, get down here."

Ignatz, a puzzled look on his face, stood next to Stevo. He looked at Stevo, whose blue eyes were troubled. His handsome mustached face under the light brown hair was a mask of concern.

Tomo, his dark brown hair uncombed, hurried down the spiral staircase, buttoning his shirt as he descended.

"What's up?" he asked. He lost his smile when he saw the stern look on Stevo's face. Tomo looked from Stevo to Ignatz. Ignatz, who was practically a family member, only shrugged his shoulders, not knowing why Stevo was there.

Stevo blurted out, "Stefan is here."

Bewildered, Tomo asked, "Stefan who?"

Ignatz stepped back, an unhappy look on his face. The man said, "No, it can't be."

Stevo turned to Ignatz, who worked for him ever since Stefan abandoned him in Gary. "Yes, Stefan is at the Dalmatcia." said Stevo.

Tomo started to ask again, "Stefan who?" Then it hit him. He almost shouted the words, "Not Stefan Vladeslav!"

Stevo nodded, yes.

Ignatz reached for a bottle of slivovitza and three glasses. The three friends, all who had reason to dislike Stefan Vladeslav, sat at the small table which was always reserved for Tomo.

Stevo already with an unlit cigarette in his hand dropped the pack of Camels on the table. He lit his cigarette, watching as Ignatz poured the slivovitza.

Tomo raised his glass in a silent toast, took a swallow and asked, "What do you suppose brought him here?"

In a low, sad voice, Stevo said, "He is here to see Barbra."

Ignatz said in a stunned whisper, "Boze moi…My God."

His brown eyes wide, Tomo asked, "Why? And how did he know she was here?"

In a flat voice, Stevo said, "Michael saw him in Marshall Fields and told him."

Both Tomo and Ignatz asked in unison, "Why?"

Stevo explained, "Michael called me yesterday. He told me that Stefan bought the painting of Barbra and asked questions about her. Not knowing who Stefan was or his relationship to Barbra, Michael told him that Barbra was in New Orleans…and that she lived in a courtyard on Canal Street."

His voice full of concern, Tomo asked, "What are we going to do?"

Ignatz was rubbing his chin, a worried look in his eyes.

In a weary voice, Stevo, his eyes watery, said, "Nothing. We will do nothing."

Tomo almost shouted, "What do you mean nothing? You and Barbra are together now. It is as if you are married."

Stevo said with the heartbreak evident in his voice, "Barbra is his legal wife."

Tomo was out of his chair, anger and frustration in his manner. He said, "Well, he didn't think of Barbra as his wife when he married Adele Manning, who, by the way, you dated before you married Katya."

Stevo, standing, took his glass and finished the drink. He looked pale and worried. "I'm going back to the hotel." He said. "Whatever happens, it will be up to Barbra." He looked at his two friends saying, "You see, I don't know what she felt for Stefan or how much."

CHAPTER 8

In his hotel room, after all the time spent on the train, Stefan undressed and bathed. Without dressing, he stretched out on the bed, soon dozing while enjoying the pleasant breeze wafting in through his open doorway at the ornate wrought iron balcony.

He awoke to the chattering of a bright colored bird on the balcony, finding bugs to eat in the decorative pots of flowering magnolias.

Running his fingers through his hair and feeling the stubble on his chin, he realized he needed to do some serious grooming, if he was to go out and find Barbra.

Before dressing, he ordered coffee and a sweet roll to be brought to his room.

Barbra was in his thoughts. He was not sorry that he had married Adele. The contacts made through Adele helped Stefan to now have more money than he ever had in the past. Tips on investments and winning at cards with some of the wealthiest businessmen gave Stefan an advantage he never would have had if he were not with Adele.

When the tray with his order arrived, instead of a sweet roll, there were beignets and chicory coffee. Both were something he had never tasted until that morning. He was pleasantly surprised at how much he enjoyed the taste of the coffee and the square fried dough sprinkled with powdered sugar.

As he dressed, he noticed a card on the dresser describing the amenities available in the hotel. The mention of the barbershop on the second floor caught his attention.

Dressing in a light tan-colored suit, a pale green tie over a cream-colored shirt, Stefan went to find the barbershop.

In the barbershop, he was greeted politely and seated in an empty chair. He was asked his room number, as that is how he was to be charged for his visit.

The man lathering his face was not a talkative person, which Stefan appreciated. He disliked small talk with strangers.

While in the chair, Stefan could not help overhearing the conversation between the barber and the older gray-haired man in the chair next to his.

The young barber was saying to the older man, "Thank you for the advice on investing. I don't have much, but I was able to buy in some bananas coming into port. I didn't make a lot of money, but I did alright."

The grey-haired man said, "If you can keep the profit and add to it, to make it grow, you'll do well."

When Stefan's shave was completed, he tipped the barber, then headed down the stairs to the main floor. Along the way, he passed the room reserved for men where they could drink, play cards, and not have to worry about their conversation shocking any women.

On the main floor, Stefan again glanced at the outdoor dining area, deciding he would eat there later in the day.

Passing the front desk, he paused to ask Louis, the day clerk, "Where is Mr. Markovich?"

Louis looked around saying, "I don't see him and I know he is not in his office. I could have him paged for you."

"Don't bother. I can see him later." said Stefan.

As he headed for the door, he passed the gift shop and stepped inside for some cigarettes. It was a very nice shop, with items of quality rather than typical cheap souvenirs.

The display of tobacco items was impressive. There were cigars, tins of tobacco for pipes, and tins of tobacco with papers for rolling one's own cigarettes.

Stefan noticed the popular brands of cigarettes in tins, such as Camels, Chesterfield, and Lucky Strikes. He preferred the Turkish cigarettes, Murads or the most popular cigarette in the country at that time, Fatima, with a veiled beautiful woman on the package.

Just beyond the gift shop was Michael DuKane's studio and gallery. Stefan admired the paintings. Some were of women or children and a few were of the city of New Orleans.

Next to Stefan stood the same white-haired man he had seen in the nearby chair in the barbershop. The man said, "We are all very proud of Michael."

Stefan turned to look at the older handsome man. He asked, "Do you know him?"

The man smiled, saying, "Ever since he was a child. His parents would come from France to do some business in New Orleans and at our bank." The old man chuckled saying, "And now he is married to my niece."

Stefan overlooked the comment about Michael being married to the man's niece. He was interested when he heard the word bank. Stefan asked, "Could you tell me where the First National Bank is? I had some money transferred from Chicago to that bank."

The white-haired man extended his hand to Stefan saying, "I am Harold Brouchard. I work at that bank. I am waiting for my carriage to take me there."

"I am Stefan Vladeslav." He shook Brouchard's hand. "Would you wait for me?" asked Stefan. "I have a brief case in my room with some papers that should be in the bank vault."

"Go ahead." said Brouchard. "I can wait."

Stefan ran to his room on the fourth floor as fast as he could. Finding his briefcase hidden in the shoe drawer of his wardrobe trunk, he hurried out of his room to join Brouchard.

He found Brouchard outside the hotel entrance standing beside a horse-drawn carriage. Brouchard motioned for Stefan to climb in. Once Brouchard was settled in the carriage, his personal driver didn't need instructions, but started toward the business center of town.

At the bank, Brouchard was the first to leave the carriage. He waived the driver on. The driver knew to wait for the banker and found a shady spot and some water for his horse. From the shaded spot, he could see the bank entrance when he was needed for a ride back to the Dalmatcia.

Inside the bank, Stefan saw several desks, enclosed with low wooden railings, sectioning them off as private areas. Everyone greeted Harold Brouchard as he and Stefan went to the far end of the room to another wooden-railed enclosure.

"Sit down." said Brouchard, motioning towards a chair, opposite the one the banker sat in.

Stefan's eyes widened when he saw the brass sign on the desk reading: Bank President. Stefan had been in enough offices of the Steel Mill executives to recognize the Bronze Tiffany Zodiac desk set displayed on the top of Brouchard's desk.

Stefan was impressed with the Banker's casual manner.

Brouchard offered an open cigarette box to Stefan, who declined, preferring his own Fatima cigarettes. Brouchard already was lighting one of his favorite cigars. After a couple of puffs, he said to his secretary who had a desk on the other side of the wooden rail, "Get me the information from a Chicago transfer in the name Vladeslav."

He asked Stefan, "What brings you to New Orleans? Planning on doing business here? We have some men from the North who are doing well here."

As the secretary handed a manila folder to Brouchard, he said, "For instance, the Dalmatcia Hotel."

Stefan leaning back in his chair, crossing his legs said, "I did see someone I knew briefly there."

Spreading the papers on his desk, Brouchard asked, "Really who might that be?"

"Stevo…Steve Markovich."

"Ah yes, I have known Steve since the day he came here." said Brouchard, "He is a good man."

"It was kind of you to get him a job there." said Stefan.

Brouchard laid the papers on the desk. The old man's surprised look confused Stefan. The banker said, "I didn't get him the job." His burst of laughter causing heads to turn in his direction. "Steve owns the Dalmatcia."

Now it was Stefan's turn to look surprised, but it was more of a stunned look than a surprised one. "I had no idea he had that kind of money." said Stefan. "I saw his store in Gary and it was rather modest. He even did funerals."

"How is it you knew him in Gary?" asked Brouchard.

Stefan stubbed his cigarette out in a crystal ashtray on the desk, saying, "He was married to my cousin. But when I got to Gary, she had already passed away."

"Katya? You were related to Katya?" Brouchard's eyes glistened with interest.

Stefan asked, "How is it you knew her?"

"I didn't but I have seen a portrait of her. Michael painted a picture of her." said Brouchard.

"That's impossible." said Stefan, "He never saw her."

Then it hit him. He remembered the long portrait, full size in Marshall Fields with a girl resembling Katya dressed in a blue gown.

Before Stefan could tell Brouchard about the painting in Chicago, the banker said, "You won't believe this, but Katya came to Michael in a dream. He painted it from his dream. Then he painted another one for Steve. It hangs in his office."

Stefan reached in his pocket for his cigarette case, saying "This is all so confusing." He shook his head in wonder as he said, "Michael painting a picture from a dream and Steve having money to buy a hotel."

Brouchard said, "Well, when he came home. I say home because he owns a house here in New Orleans. He came here from some village when he was fourteen with his father. I knew his father well."

He placed his cigar in the ashtray, saying, "Let's see what you want to put in our safe. I have an appointment this afternoon."

They spent about half an hour going over Stefan's papers and opening an account for him with the money sent from the Chicago bank. When everything was completed, receipts written out and papers signed, the two went out as the carriage was almost at the door.

The two men chatted pleasantly, easily enjoying each other's company. When they arrived at the entrance of the Dalmatcia, Brouchard said to Stefan, "I want you to meet my driver and my very good friend, Bobo Johnson. He knows New Orleans well and will take you wherever you want to go"

Bobo turned and with a cool stare at Stefan said, "Mr. Brouchard, I have met this man. I have heard him complain that Mr. Steve's place was not what he expected. He complained that Mr. Steve did not have an automobile."

Stefan was surprised as he recognized Bobo, the Black man who worked for Stevo, and he felt his cheeks reddening.

Then Bobo said, "And I was there on that wet, rainy day at the Gary Hotel when you walked right past Miss Barbra as if she was invisible. But, worst of all, I was with Miss Barbra the day she found out you done married the woman you were with at the Gary Hotel."

Then Bobo looked at Mr. Brouchard saying, "I don't want to drive this man anywhere. He left Miss Barbra alone in Zagreb and when she followed him to Gary he walked right passed her, like he didn't know her."

Brouchard, ever the Southern gentleman, said to Stefan in a soft, polite voice, "I am sorry. I thought we might be friends, but now I don't think so. I will have your banking account turned over to a very capable associate." Mr. Brouchard politely tipped his panama straw hat and left Stefan staring after him. At the same time, Bobo flicked his whip and drove the carriage away, leaving Stefan standing confused and feeling ashamed.

CHAPTER 9

A somewhat disappointed Harold Brouchard entered the lobby of the Dalmatcia hotel. He nodded a greeting to those he passed, not stopping to chat, wanting to find Stevo.

At the front desk, he asked the young clerk, Louis, "Is Steve available?"

Louis nodded towards the dining area saying, "I believe I just saw him go in for lunch."

As Harold neared the table, Stevo politely started to rise, but Harold with a motion of his hand stopped him.

Stevo asked, "Have you had lunch?"

Sitting across from Stevo, the banker asked, "What are you having?"

"Just some sausage with red beans and rice." replied Stevo, noticing that Brouchard appeared to be in a serious mood.

A waiter was presently at the table taking the food order. When they were alone, Stevo asked, "Is something wrong?"

Ignoring the question, Brouchard took a drink of water. As he placed the glass on the table, he said to Stevo, "Tell me Steve, how is it that you and Tom, Ignatz, Barbra, and Josef, when he was alive, are like one family? Even Bobo and Cleona are like family to all of you."

Stevo wasn't sure why Brouchard asked this question. He pulled a pack of Camels from his pocket and studied the older man while lighting his cigarette. "You have known us for quite some time. Why are you asking this question now?"

"Because I have family here in New Orleans, and am not as close to them as I am to all of you. None of you are related, yet you are a family."

Stevo puffed his cigarette, blew smoke into the air, thinking how to answer what seemed a strange question.

"Harold," he began, "You live in a house that your grandfather built in the mid 1800s. You grew up there and you still do."

"What does that have to do with my question?' asked Brouchard.

The conversation stopped as the waiter brought the tray with the rice and beans along with a basket of bread. The two men waited as their water glasses were being refilled before Stevo tried to answer the man who was like a father to him.

Stevo picked up his fork saying, "You belong here. Even the people in New Orleans who are not related to you, are part of who you are." Stevo put his fork back on the table as he continued with his explanation.

"Those of us who left everything behind and came to America, not knowing the language, not having friends, were frightened and lonely in a way you may not understand."

Stevo looked up at the flowering trees in the outdoor garden and paused a moment before continuing. He said, "When I first came here, hearing someone speaking Croatian I would smile, even though I did not know the person speaking. It was a connection to home."

Stevo went on talking, letting his food get cold, "When I passed someone who reminded me of someone back in Dalmatcia, I would get a warm feeling. Then I would go to bars or restaurants where many Croatians would gather. And…most of them felt just like I did. We didn't bond with everyone, but some of us would feel comfortable with one another. Then we would become more than casual friends."

Stevo looked at Harold, wondering if the man understood what he was trying to say. "We would go to weddings, to Christenings, any celebration where we could all gather and feel comradeship."

"Eat your food." said Brouchard, "It is getting cold."

Stevo took a bite of food, his eyes on his friend. After a few moments of silence, he asked, "Why these questions? You never asked about our close relationships with each other before."

Before speaking, Brouchard wiped his mouth with his napkin. He said, "Tell me about Stefan Vladeslav."

Stevo was stunned by the question. He swallowed what he had in his mouth and asked in a surprised tone, "How do you know Stefan?"

Looking serious, Brouchard said, "I spent some time with him at the bank. He transferred some money from Chicago to New Orleans. He also wanted to store some papers in our vault."

Stevo didn't say anything, he was so surprised. He just stared at Brouchard waiting for more explanation.

The banker took his last forkful of rice and chewed. When he had finished, he put down his fork and look into Stevo's eyes. He said, "Bobo doesn't like this Vladeslav man. He told me about Barbra being left in Zagreb and how Vladeslav ignored her when she came to Gary."

Stevo pushed his plate aside saying, "When Barbra and Josef arrived I got a call from the concierge at the Gary Hotel that they were waiting for Stefan. Bobo and I went to pick them up."

Stevo shook his head as if he still didn't understand how Stefan could ignore Barbra and walk right pass her with Adele. He had admired Barbra's strength when she showed no recognition of him.

He said to Brouchard, "Barbra never said a word when Stefan ignored her, but she did get a bit pale."

The waiter poured coffee for both men and Stevo continued saying, "Bobo and I took Barbra and Josef to my store, where I had living quarters above. We gave Barbra Stefan's room and had another for Josef."

Stevo sipped his coffee. The look on his face was one of sadness as he remembered that day and how badly he felt for Barbra. He said, "Stefan never returned, though we did expect him. If Barbra cried, we didn't see it."

Watching the waiter place a coffee carafe on the table Brouchard cut the end of his 10-cent William Penn Cigar, lit it, and waited patiently for the waiter to leave.

"Tell me," he said, "Did Barbra and Josef have anything going on between them while in Zagreb? I only ask because it may explain why Stefan left her there."

Stevo toyed with his coffee cup. He kept his eyes on the table when he replied, "According to Ignatz, who lived and worked with them at their store, Josef was only Barbra's doctor. If he had any feeling for her then, he never indicated it. Barbra had two miscarriages and Stefan blamed Barbra for the loss of each boy baby."

Now Brouchard's face showed concern.

Stevo continued, "Also, according to Ignatz, the antique store was a success because of Barbra and her expertise. Stefan could not describe the merchandise or buy anything that was offered to him." Stevo spread his hands out saying, "So, Stefan, realizing the success of his business was all due to Barbra, began to resent her and was not always kind to her."

Brouchard puffed thoughtfully on his cigar. He said, "I was hoping you would tell me something that might make me want to be his friend. Now, I think I am even more disappointed than when Bobo told me about him."

The banker let out a big sigh. "Why do you suppose he is here? When I heard he had been in Gary, I thought he was part of your clan."

Stevo's eyes showed great sadness as he said, "He is here for Barbra. After all, she is still his wife."

CHAPTER 10

After Bobo had left and Harold Brouchard went into the Dalmatcia, Stefan stood in front of the hotel, undecided about going in and having some lunch. He didn't want to see the banker again. Not yet.

He stood on the walkway, out of the way of the incoming carriages. As he looked around, he saw the building across the street with block letters spelling LITTLE ZAGREB.

From the outside, he could not determine if it was a restaurant, but he noticed people going in, so he followed.

He stepped aside as some people were exiting before he entered a newly-painted white-walled room with a typical red stenciled border design at the top of the wall. He could smell the fresh paint and see tables covered in white cloth with again the Croatian red hand-embroidered edging on the cloth.

Stefan was quite pleased with this room. He noticed a spiral metal staircase leading to an upper level, wondering what was up there.

"Sit wherever you want." said a plump woman wearing an ankle-length white skirt. Over it was a long blue cotton apron. Her long-sleeved blouse was white as was the scarf covering her hair tied at the back at her neck.

Stefan looked around the room at the different sized tables. Some were round, some square, and along a side wall was a larger rectangular table.

Stefan chose a small round table near the center of the room. The bare center of the room was what Stefan assumed to be a dance floor.

The woman said to Stefan, "Today I have sarma... stuffed cabbage rolls, krumpir...potatoes. Stefan interrupted her saying, "The sarma will be fine."

69

As the woman turned to walk to the kitchen, a man appeared with a bottle of red wine and a glass. Stefan had not ordered the wine and was a little surprised to see that it was being put on the table. He looked at the man who brought the wine and his jaw dropped. He was so surprised that for a moment he could not speak.

Ignatz poured the wine from the bottle into a glass saying, "I remember that you liked red wine with your meals."

Stefan noticed that Ignatz no longer behaved like the servant he had been to Stefan. Ignatz, during the two years since Stefan last saw him, had acquired the confidence of a man who held a position of some importance. He was almost totally in charge of running the Little Zagreb establishment. He did the hiring, oversaw that the women in the kitchen did their job well, while doing most of the ordering of food and beverages.

Stefan was nearly speechless. It took him a moment to compose himself. In a few moments he said to the smiling Ignatz, "So, Stevo owns this place too and you work for him."

A man descending the spiral staircase said, "No, he works for me and I own this place."

Looking up, Stefan recognized Tomo, the young man who, in Gary, worked for Stevo and who Stefan had not liked. Stefan had considered Tomo just a servant, not the family-like employee that Stevo felt him to be.

Tomo saw someone entering the restaurant that he wanted to speak with. Without excusing himself, and without so much as a nod, Tomo went to his private table where Bronko Yelich, the winemaker from Triumph, stood waiting for him.

Bronko was a stocky man with a full head of brown hair. On his tanned face were dark eyes framed with bushy brown eyebrows. Whenever Bronko came to New Orleans, his plain blue shirt and black pants were always clean.

Stefan asked Ignatz, who was still standing at the table, "Who is that man with Tomo?"

Without waiting to be invited, Ignatz pulled out a chair and sat opposite Stefan. He said, "That is the man who made the wine I just poured for you."

Now Ignatz put another glass he had in his hand on the table and poured some wine into it. He turned towards the table where Tomo and Bronko sat. Catching Bronko's attention, Ignatz raised his glass in a toast to the winemaker, who returned the gesture with a wide smile and a nod of his head.

Stefan sniffed the wine before taking a sip. He was pleasantly surprised and said to Ignatz, "This is good wine. Where is that man from?"

Ignatz took another sip of the red wine before saying, "Originally from Dalmatcia, but now from Triumph, which is in another parish."

"Parish? You mean on land owned by a church?"

The lady in the blue apron placed a plate of stuffed cabbage rolls and potatoes in front of him. "Oh, this smells wonderful." he said before Ignatz could reply.

Ignatz watched as Stefan took a fork full of the sarma. Between bites, Stefan said, "I haven't had this since we left Zagreb. It is delicious."

Smiling, Ignatz said, "Here in Louisiana, different areas are called parishes. There are towns and cities in each of the parishes."

At his table, Tomo tapped his ring against a wine bottle to get Ignatz's attention. Without a word to Stefan, Ignatz got up going to Tomo's private table.

While Stefan was enjoying his meal, he also enjoyed the sounds of tambura music performed by two young men at the back of the room. They weren't really giving a performance. They just enjoyed playing their string instruments.

The woman who served Stefan asked, "Do you know Ignatz?"

Stefan looked at the woman. She was a combination of all the women he knew back home in Vladezemla. He felt so comfortable in this place named Little Zagreb.

"Yes." He said. "I know Ignatz very well. We were together in Zagreb."

"I am called Klara." she said. "I don't see Ignatz sit with people. I knew you must be someone special." She left going back into the kitchen area.

Klara! Her name is Klara. That was the name of the housekeeper from the time he had been a young child back in Vladezemla.

Stefan looked around the room again. The stenciled designs on the walls, the smell of the food, the men playing their tamburas...it was as if he were back home on his father's land.

Klara was back with a plate of orenjace...nut roll and a cup of the black coffee with the grounds in the bottom of the cup. He smiled seeing the nut roll. He looked at the coffee and then looked up at Klara standing next to him. She said nothing, just looked at him. He looked at the coffee and then looked back at her. He gave Klara a small smile, saying "You are going to tell my fortune aren't you?"

With a smile and not quite a wink, she walked away.

Two more men with string instruments walked past Stefan's table, nodding politely as they passed him.

Soon there were four men playing music that was so familiar to him.

He felt as if he were home with his neighbors. He felt as if he was among his people, the people that at one time, he couldn't wait to leave.

When Ignatz returned to the table, Stefan said, "I would like to meet that man." He meant the winemaker.

"Maybe another time." said Ignatz, "He wants to leave and needs to find his sister, Alta."

Ignatz had to leave the table. The room was filling up with people. Men alone and some couples. The music and the conversations gave the room a livelier atmosphere.

Klara was back at Stefan's table. Seeing that he had finished the coffee, she turned the cup upside down on the saucer then walked away.

The wine bottle was still on the table so Stefan poured more into his glass. He took his cigarette case from his pocket and pulled out one of his favorite, Fatima cigarettes. He lit up the cigarette watching all the activity going on in the room.

To his surprise, Klara, came and sat at the table. She picked up the cup and studied the design left by the dripping coffee grounds on the inside of the cup. She looked inside the cup and then she looked at Stefan, saying nothing.

After a moment, smiling he asked, "What is my fortune going to cost me?"

Smiling back at him, seeing his cigarette case on the table, she said, "One of those cigarettes."

He laughed as he opened the case and let her pick out a cigarette.

"Take another." he said.

Klara put the two cigarettes on the table top in front of her.

Stefan studied her face. It was a strong face. It was a face that showed a life of hardship. Still he could tell that once she had been a beauty.

Klara looked into the cup again. There was no smile now. Her eyes moved from the cup to Stefan's face.

She said her voice low and serious, "You are going to need all the strength you have to face your future. There is a woman who will change the way you live and the way you want to live."

CHAPTER 11

After Klara removed the dishes, Stefan sat at the table for some time. He listened to the music, caught snatches of conversations in his native Croatian, heard friendly laughter, and felt comfortable in the room.

The regular patrons nodded at the handsome, well-dressed Stefan, wondering who he was.

Tomo left his table to go upstairs a couple times while Ignatz, constantly on the move, was in the kitchen, in the bar area, and or the dining area.

Stefan didn't see Klara, so he motioned to another server. He asked for a bill. This much slimmer woman left to find Klara who told her that the handsome man was Ignatz's guest so there was no charge.

Stefan was more than a little surprised, not to mention moved by the fact that his once servant, was now buying him a meal and wine. He looked around the room for Ignatz to thank him, but didn't see him.

It was late afternoon and Stefan didn't realize the day had passed so quickly. While on the train, he imagined that on his first day in New Orleans he would find Barbra. He was sure he could win her back. He wondered if Josef had gone back to Zagreb.

On the street, he felt the excitement of the city. He watched as people hurried as they walked and he wondered where they were going. On the street ahead of him, he heard singing. He followed the sound. A Black man was playing a clarinet while another was lightly tapping a drum. A very slim and beautiful Black woman, in a shiny, green dress was singing *Ballin' the Jack*. Passersby tossed coins in a small wicker basket. She smiled and thanked them, then went on to the sing the lively *Abba Dabba Honeymoon*.

Nearby, Stefan heard the sound of a woman's voice. It sounded as if she was struggling and arguing. To Stefan's surprise, the yelling he heard was in the Croatian language. He walked to where the sounds became louder. Stefan found that he was at the back of the Dalmatcia, near the kitchen entrance. There he saw a man struggling with a blond woman, who appeared not to want to go with the man. Just then the door to the back of the hotel opened and Stevo came out.

When the woman saw Stevo, she stopped struggling. He said to her, "What do you want, Alta? You know I don't want to see you."

Stefan stayed back, hidden by a large pink Formosa azalea bush.

Now, Stefan recognized the man arguing with her. It was Bronko Yelich, the winemaker he had seen in Little Zagreb.

Bronko apologized to Stevo. "I didn't know she was in the wagon until we were half way here. I'm sorry. You know I didn't want her to come here."

Stevo looked at Alta, the woman he thought he loved a year ago, until he discovered she thought him to be wealthy and a great catch. Bronko had warned Stevo that Alta had been flirting with other men, hoping to marry someone with money.

"Stevo," said Bronko. "We need to unload the wine and I want to get back on the road while I still have some light." He spread his hands out as if he didn't know what to do. He said, "Maybe we can lock her in a room somewhere."

Alta struggled against her brother's grip. She said, "I will scream so loud they will hear me all the way in Triumph."

Without much thought, Stefan stepped out from behind the azalea bush, surprising Stevo and the winemaker.

He made a small polite bow to Bronko saying, "I saw you in Little Zagreb and Ignatz introduced me to your very good wine."

Stevo frowned, not happy to have to introduce him to Bronko. He said, "Bronko, this is Stefan Vladeslav. He was my Katya's cousin." To Stefan he said, "This is Bronko Yelich, who makes the only wine we serve at the Dalmatcia."

Stevo noticed that Alta had calmed down considerably. She straightened her long blue dress then ran her hand over her blond hair, fashioned in a bun at the back of her head. Most of all, Stevo noticed that she had fixed her dark eyes onto Stefan's eyes. He remembered that she always did that to him when they were together.

Now Alta's angry face relaxed into a soft pleasant smile which was directed at Stefan.

Bronko exchanged a look with Stevo, both recognizing that Alta was at work using her charms on Stefan.

Stefan recognized flirtation when he saw it. He had spent a good deal of his youth, during his school years in Zagreb, at Magda's Gambling house. He also spent a lot of time upstairs with the available girls offering their charms for money.

Stefan made a polite bow to Alta saying, "I would be very pleased to keep company with you at the Little Zagreb while your brother and Stevo complete their business."

Alta reached out her hand to Stefan, while giving Stevo and her brother a smug, confident glare. "I would love to go with you." she said. "You are such a gentleman."

Before Bronko could protest, Stevo said, "Thank you, Stefan, we should be done within an hour."

Taking Alta's hand, he put it on his arm saying, "No need to hurry."

Stefan and Alta slowly walked away towards Little Zagreb.

Bronko started to say something, but Stevo stopped him saying, "Anything Alta does to him, he deserves."

Bronko didn't know what this remark meant, but if Stevo didn't care, than neither would he.

Activity in Little Zagreb was much livelier than it had been when Stefan left. Many curious eyes looked at the handsome stranger and the beautiful woman with him as he was guided to the same table he had earlier.

Alta liked this place. It was full of activity and music. Most of all, it was full of men.

Klara was almost immediately at the table. She glanced at Alta then looked Stefan directly in his face. He almost laughed because it was the same look the housekeeper, Klara, from his youth would have given him when she had been displeased.

To Alta, Klara said, "We just made some palachinke seer or slatke….Crepes with cheese or sweet jelly."

Alta said, "The sweet palachinke and some coffee."

Without a word, Klara looked at Stefan, who said, "Coffee with milk and more of the orenjace…nut roll."

Alta's eyes were dancing with pleasure. What a lively place this was compared to the rural life she lived on the vineyard in Triumph. She tapped her fingers on the table to the song, *Marianna,* being sung by two men at the far end of the room, playing their string instruments, a prima and a brach.

Soon people in the room joined in to sing the song. Singing was in the hearts of most Croatians and they never missed an opportunity to sing when the moment came.

Stefan took his cigarette case from his suit coat pocket. As he opened the gold case, he noticed Alta's eyes were fixed on it. He offered the open case for her to take a cigarette, but she shook her head not wanting one. It was not the cigarettes she wanted. She was impressed by the gold case.

Stefan removed three cigarettes. He left two cigarettes on the table and lit the third for himself. He reached into his trouser pocket and pulled out a Morgan silver dollar.

Alta watched as he picked up the two cigarettes placing them in the same hand as the silver dollar.

Klara was at the table with a tray. She didn't smile or say a word as she put the crepes in front of Alta. Next, she put the cups of coffee on the table.

Klara, wearing the same blue apron she wore earlier when she served Stefan his lunch, was surprised to see him drop something in her apron pocket. With her free hand, she pulled the pocket lightly open to look in. Now, she smiled.

Alta cut her crepe with the side of her fork. She put the food in her mouth, again fixing her eyes on Stefan's eyes. He knew what she was doing and found it entertaining. He knew that she was aware that she was beautiful and no doubt was adept at playing with men. He deliberately looked away, concentrating on the musicians in the back of the room. He made it a point of looking at women who passed by their table, further confusing Alta and annoying her.

Ignatz, passing the table, was surprised to see Stefan back so soon and with Alta. He and Tomo knew about Alta.

Stefan grabbed Ignatz's hand asking, "Do you ever see Barbra?"

Ignatz pulled his hand away only saying, "I have seen her around." He was not going to give Stefan any more information. Stefan didn't need to know that Ignatz was almost a part of Barbra's family. Neither did Stefan need to know how much those who came from Gary meant to one another.

Alta watched as Ignatz, saying no more, walked away. She asked, "Who is Barbra, a relative or an old sweetheart?"

Stefan didn't need to answer. Bronko was behind Alta, saying, "Let's go. I am finished here."

Alta's pretty face hardened and her dark eyes showed annoyance.

Stefan stood. He went to Alta and moved her chair so she could get up.

"Get in the wagon." said her brother, as she started to ask Stefan if she would see him again.

Stefan ignored Alta and stopped Bronko as he started towards the door. He asked the stocky man, "There were grape vines on my father's land and some of the people made wine. Could I visit your vineyard and see how you do things there?"

In an exasperated tone, Bronko said, "You don't have to make up an excuse to see Alta. If you want to come see her, then do so."

Alta was already out the door out of hearing range. Stefan took hold of Bronko's arm, saying, "I want to see your land and your winery. I won't come if you don't want me to."

Bronko looked into Stefan's eyes. He believed that Stefan was sincere when he asked to see the winery. "Come anytime." He said.

Stefan went back to the table to finish his coffee and slice of nut roll.

Klara was at the table to remove Alta's dishes. She looked at Stefan, saying, "That is not a good woman."

Stefan let out a laugh so loud, it made heads turn. He said to Klara, "You could be my kuma or teta...godmother or aunt. You make me feel as if I am home in Vladeszemla."

With a napkin in her free hand, she brushed away the crumbs on the table. Before she turned to walk back to the kitchen, she paused looking at Stefan. She said, "When it comes to beautiful women, men can be so dumb!"

CHAPTER 12

The next morning, Stefan awoke feeling wonderful.

On the dresser, propped against the wall was Michael DuKane's portrait of Barbra.

He leaned his elbows on the dresser and stared at the portrait of the woman he had abandoned. He was sure that now that he had found her, they would be just as they had been when they were first married and so much in love. Though he had not really seen her, he felt as if they were together. It was only a matter of finding the courtyard on Canal Street and, for Stefan, another life in America would begin.

Stefan washed. Rather than go to the barber shop, he shaved himself. His reflection in the mirror showed him smiling. He was very pleased.

Despite his unpleasant parting from the bank president, Mr. Brouchard, Stefan felt the rest of the day had been successful.

Dressed in light tan gabardine trousers and a cream-colored shirt with a maroon and grey striped tie, Stefan felt good. He carried his suit jacket, walking down the stairs to the outdoor eating area.

In the lobby and in the restaurant, he did not see Stevo or Brouchard.

When the server brought a menu, Stefan said, "Some strong coffee and bring whatever is a popular breakfast here."

As the server left Stefan's table, another was there with a large cup of steaming coffee. There were also beignets, which Stefan assumed were given with coffee in the morning to everyone.

He was seated at a nice outdoor table for two surrounded by flowers and cages of birds. Bird cages were at various locations in the dining area. There was something comforting with the sounds of the chirping birds. One small flying white bird landed on the floor next to Stefan's table. The bird looked up at Stefan. He smiled thinking this bird was used to finding food here. Stefan broke off a piece of his beignet, crumbling it and dropping the crumbs on the stone paved ground. There were chirps from the bird as it picked at the crumbs.

Stefan admired the flowers while sipping his delicious coffee. He was impressed by the people he saw coming and going in the dining area. All were so very polite and proper, speaking softly, nodding to him as they passed his table.

It wasn't long before the waiter brought a plate which he placed before Stefan. Looking at the plate, Stefan asked, "What is this?"

The server politely replied, "This is a typical breakfast of sautéed pork and vegetables over fried yellow grits." The young man stood waiting for some response from Stefan before saying, "If you would rather I bring you something else, I am happy to do so."

"No, no." said Stefan. "This is fine. Thank you."

Stefan took a forkful of the yellow cornmeal and was pleasantly surprised. It was polenta, just as he had it when he was home in Vladezemla.

While eating breakfast, Stefan watched the people around him. Right then, he was sure that he was going to be happy in New Orleans.

Remembering last evening, Stefan wasn't sure why he wanted to be friends with Bronko Yelich. He liked the man and he liked Bronko's wine. And, most of all, he wanted to see a real winery.

With his meal finished and the dishes cleared, Stefan enjoyed another cup of coffee and a cigarette. He decided that he liked the different tasting coffee served in New Orleans.

Leaving a generous tip for the server, Stefan left the dining area. He put on his suit coat, stopping at the reception desk.

"How do I get to Canal Street?" he asked the clerk behind the desk.

Louis, the clerk he had met before, said, "You can get a carriage or a cab to take you there. If you prefer to walk, just keep going straight out the hotel doors until you see a street with streetcar rails. That will be Canal Street."

Stefan thanked Louis. While heading for the doors, he made a stop at the hotel gift shop and again purchased his Fatima cigarettes.

Outdoors, a gentle floral-scented breeze made Stefan's walk a pleasant one. He passed by several people washing the sidewalks in front of their establishments. Stefan smiled as he saw, against a wall, a low to the sidewalk drinking water reservoir for dogs.

Everyone he passed on his walk, of every color, politely smiled when passing him. He found this so very pleasant. He could pass a hundred people in Chicago and only occasionally get a friendly nod.

As he walked, he was aware of the European charm of New Orleans. Street vendors, women selling flowers with baskets of fruit on their heads reminded him of the market in Zagreb where women sold their flowers, produce, and handmade items.

Ahead, he saw the streetcar tracks. The sign on the pole read, Canal Street. His heart started to race as he heard the clanging of the streetcar, signaling to him that he was near Barbra.

His Barbra! He was ashamed for having left her alone in Zagreb. He felt the shame of ignoring her in Gary. Stefan wondered, was Josef still with her, or had he returned to Zagreb?

Stefan walked along Canal Street, looking for the courtyard Michael DuKane had described. He passed many courtyards, several with iron gates, but so far none as large as he was looking for.

Thinking he should have gotten a better description or even an address, Stefan stood in front of a large-entranced courtyard. Close to the entrance was a circular garden, with a roadway around it for carriages to easily pass. Inside, he saw a young girl with dark curls pulling a smaller boy of perhaps two or three years old in a wagon.

Slowly, Stefan entered the yard. He saw a large house to the left with a wrought iron balcony. To the back was a two-story building which he thought to be a carriage house with living quarters above. To his right he saw a small cottage with a patio area. There were chairs and a round table.

When he saw her, Stefan felt as if he had been slapped in the face! Under the shade of a large umbrella was his Barbra. She had a baby at her bare breast, her head down as she looked at the nursing baby.

Stefan swayed at the sight. She had a baby! She had someone else's baby after two of his babies with her had ended in miscarriages!

He stood in the entrance too stunned to move until the dark-haired girl pulling the wagon stood in front of him.

"Hello." she said. "I am Kate. Did you want to see my uncle? He isn't here."

Behind the girl came a thin Black woman. The scowl on her face showed her displeasure at seeing Stefan. He didn't recognize Cleona. In Gary he had no interest in Stevo's employees.

"What you doin' here?" she demanded. "We don't need you here and we don't want you here."

Cleona had been in business with Stevo's wife, Katya. Cleona was a part of the Gary family as was her cousin, Bobo.

From behind Cleona, Barbra asked, "What is it, Cleona? Is something wrong?"

Stefan pushed past Cleona. He walked around Kate pulling the boy in the wagon. He stood in front of Barbra, staring at her.

The color went out of Barbra's face. *Dear God, it can't be Stefan!*

They each stared at one another, speechless.

Stefan could not believe his eyes seeing Barbra nursing a baby. She had miscarried two of his babies and now…she had a baby at her breast, a baby that should have been his.

Cleona was at Barbra's side. She gathered up the baby with one arm and draped a towel over Barbra's bare breast.

Standing behind Barbra, Cleona rocked the baby, who appeared to be almost asleep.

Barbra pulled the top of her green silk robe closed, having removed the towel covering her breast while placing it on a side table.

Little Kate and the adopted Joso, were now near Barbra, curious who the stranger was. Kate especially wanted to know why Cleona told the man he wasn't wanted there.

Little Joso, sensing something was wrong, got out of the wagon and went to Barbra's side, where he leaned against her shoulder, his wide, brown eyes staring at the stranger.

This was not the reunion Stefan wanted or had expected. He had anticipated an expression of pleasure from Barbra, perhaps some emotional tears. Instead Barbra stared at him with disbelief in her eyes.

Questions filled her mind. *Why was he here? What did he want?*

Cleona stood behind Barbra, scowling at Stefan. She didn't say anything, though she wanted to let him know how little she though of him.

After what seemed like an eternity of silence, Barbra asked, her voice sounding thin, "Why have you come here?"

Without permission, Stefan sat in the chair at the table across from Barbra. Studying her face, while fighting his confusion at seeing her with children, he said in a low voice, "My plan was for us to get back together. To tell you I was so wrong in leaving for America without you. And…" He couldn't go on, because in him was a combination of anger and confusion from seeing her with children of her own.

Barbra said nothing, just looked at him. She had all sorts of conflicting emotions going on within her. She remembered the hurt and anger of being abandoned. She recalled the hurt of his blaming her for the miscarriages.

However, the most stirring memory was that she had once loved him so very much. Walking along the Trg de Republic Square in Zagreb on warm, floral-scented evenings; stopping at outdoor cafés for coffee or a sweet cake. These were such warm memories.

Then she remembered how delirious with happiness they had been with the discovery of the valuable paintings and artifacts left in the office of the building Stefan inherited from the Madam in Zagreb.

Now, here in the courtyard, Stefan lit a cigarette, silently watching Barbra's face. He broke into her thoughts as he asked, "Who is the father of your children?"

The tone of his voice and the question jolted Barbra from her sweet memories.

"Josef was the father of Joso and Gabriella." said Barbra, watching Stefan's face for a reaction. She remembered how Stefan disliked that Josef had been so caring of her when she had the miscarriages. She didn't bother to say they took Joso as their own when Joso's mother had died.

Cleona, not wanting to leave Barbra, leaned down to Kate saying, "Go get Virgine. Tell her to come get the baby."

Stefan's face hardened slightly. He took a long drag on the cigarette and blew a long plume of smoke into the air. He leaned his elbow on the table as Barbra brushed away the cigarette smoke with her hand.

He asked, "Was? Josef was the father? Has he left you?"

Barbra gave Stefan a hard stare as she said, "Yes, he left me. He didn't walk out on me like you did. He died!"

Stefan was surprised to hear Josef had died. He looked at Barbra. Saw the sunlight shine on her golden red hair, as always in the Gibson girl style. It took him a moment before he asked, "When did he die?"

"In July on the day Gabriella was born." said Barbra, studying Stefan's face.

Just then Virgine approached the table. She saw the serious looks on all the faces, especially on Cleona's face. She knew the mood was serious because no one acknowledged her. Cleona handed Gabriella to Virgine. Always, even though Virgine worked for them, she would be introduced to a guest.

Slim, light-skinned Virgine, a long white apron over her grey skirt, waited not sure what to do. A slight nod of Cleona's head indicated that Gabriella be taken into the large house where Barbra now lived.

Little Kate was back at Barbra's side, now with her arm around Barbra's shoulder.

Stefan looked around at the courtyard and then back at Barbra with the children pressed against her. His mind couldn't grasp what he was seeing. He had such wonderful thoughts of finding Barbra and of her being so happy to see him.

"Could I have something cold to drink?" he asked.

Barbra turned to Cleona, saying, "Bring some lemonade, also for the children."

Not seeing an ashtray, Stefan snuffed his cigarette on the edge of the metal table, dropping the cigarette butt on the ground.

Kate immediately went and picked up the finished cigarette from the ground and deposited it in a flower pot.

A little surprised, Stefan asked Barbra, "Who is this little girl?"

Independent and very mature for her eight years, Little Kate stood in front of the seated Stefan. She announced, "I am Kate Brouchard and I live here in the courtyard."

Stefan hesitated a moment before asking, "Did you say your name is Brouchard?"

"Yes. And...I was born in this house." She indicated the house behind the patio.

Cleona brought a tray with glasses of lemonade which she placed on the table. Barbra served the first glass to Stefan then gave the smaller glasses to Kate and Joso, taking the last for herself.

Stefan took a long swallow of the cool drink. He studied Kate. He looked at Barbra, not understanding her connection to Brouchard.

He said, "I met a Harold Brouchard yesterday."

Kate said, "That is my grandpère."

Stefan looked confused. He watched as Barbra smoothed Joso's hair.

When she looked up at Stefan, he said, "I don't understand how it is that you know Brouchard and have his granddaughter?"

Joso was becoming bored and he climbed up nestling into Barbra's lap. Barbra said, "Kate was here when Josef and I came."

Kate cut into the conversation, "I lived here with my Uncle Steve. Over there in the big house." She pointed across the way.

Stefan looked back at the big house across from where they were sitting. Returning his gaze to Barbra he asked, "Is she talking about Stevo?"

"Yes." said Barbra with a small smile. "That house belonged to his father and when Steve came to New Orleans, it became his. Mr. Brouchard owned this house." She indicated the house behind the patio.

"So," said Stefan, "Stevo is your neighbor."

Kate giggled then said, "We all live in the big house, except Cleona. She has this house and Bobo has the house in back."

Stefan's face reddened. He asked, "You live with Stevo?"

Barbra looked directly into Stefan's eyes. "Yes, I am with Steve." she said, "And I always will be."

This was not what he wanted to hear. This meeting with Barbra had gone all wrong. He had it all worked out in his mind, but...he never expected to find Barbra with children or, worse yet, with Stevo.

He rose without a word. He didn't look at any of them as he hurried out of the courtyard into Canal Street. A streetcar was coming to a stop and he ran to it and hopped on. He didn't care where it was going. Stefan needed to get away from the courtyard and away from his disappointment.

CHAPTER 13

Stefan's mind was in a whirl. This meeting with Barbra was not what he had hoped it would be. As the streetcar made its way down Canal Street, Stefan was oblivious to the sights. He kept seeing Barbra nursing the baby that he wished had been his.

The sound of music broke into his thoughts. He became aware that the streetcar was not moving. Several people got off the streetcar to watch what Stefan thought to be a parade. It wasn't long before he realized it was a funeral procession. One like he had never seen. Back home in Vladezemla, he saw musicians follow a funeral procession, but not with the gaiety he witnessed here. Along with some others, he followed the marchers to see where they were going.

The parade stopped at what appeared to Stefan to be a field of tombs standing upright. Not just grave stones, but actual small buildings. Some he thought were for more than one deceased. Stefan had no idea that the water level was so high that in-ground burials were impossible.

Stefan walked through the beautiful cemetery until he saw a street, where he hailed a coach. "Just drive around." he told the coachmen.

As they rode around New Orleans, Stefan saw water in the distance. "Take me there." He pointed to the water where he saw the tops of boats.

At the waterfront were many carriages, wagons, and workman loading and unloading cargo from the islands. As Stefan walked around, he saw many stacks of baled cotton, assorted fruit, and some crates marked as fabric from France. He even saw stalks of bananas, not knowing that was how they grew.

He kept walking and took in sights he had never seen before. As he walked further along the dock, instead of cargo ships, he saw fishing boats. On these docks were baskets of eels, fish, crabs, and sea life he did not recognize. Old fishermen were sitting on upended barrels repairing fishing nets.

Walking past him, Stefan heard two men speaking Croatian. He watched them as they passed him, seeing they were fishermen.

Stefan followed them, pleased to hear they spoke Croatian.

He saw them enter a small wooden building. On the front of the building, Stefan recognized signs that indicated it was a café.

Stepping inside, Stefan was aware that almost everyone in the place turned to look at him. He was certainly out of place in his fine tan suit, while the patrons of this place were in various sorts of work clothes.

As Stefan looked around for a place to sit, a large man wearing a kitchen stained apron, pulled out a chair at a nearby table, saying, "Sit here."

The man offered his hand saying, "I am Mirko, cook and owner."

Stefan reached out to shake hands with Mirko, only to see that Mirko's smile turned to a frown. Seeing Stefan's gold ring with the family crest, Mirko demanded, "What you want here? You from the bank? Soon I be paid up and place is mine!"

Stunned, Stefan could only look at Mirko, speechless.

A friendly voice asked, "Stefan, what are you doing here?"

Klara, from Little Zagreb, stood beside the table.

Mirko asked, "You know this man?"

Klara laughed at Mirko saying, "Yes. I have friends you don't know."

She sat at the table across from Stefan, asking "How is it you found my cousin's place?" Before he could reply, she said to her cousin, "Bring us something to drink." She looked at Stefan, "Is pivo...beer okay?"

With a wave of her hand to her cousin, Mirko, she said, "Pivo."

Stefan reached into his suit coat pocket and pulled out his cigarette case. When opened, he offered it to Klara. Smiling she took one. He said, "Take another."

Mirko brought three beers. He sat down uninvited. After all, it was his place and his cousin knew this finely-dressed man.

He looked at Klara saying, "So you know this man?"

She smiled saying, "We are such good fiends that I told him his fortune."

Mirko asked, "What you want to eat? I cook any kind of fish you want. He waved his arm towards the wall where glass tanks of live fish swam, soon to be someone's meal.

Stefan shook his head saying, "No, Hvala...thank you."

"I be right back." said Mirko, as he headed for the back to the kitchen.

Klara and Stefan barely drank any pivo, when Mirko returned with a plate of oysters, which he proudly set on the center of the table.

Stefan's eyes widened as he said, "They are raw."

Mirko asked, "You never had oysters?"

Stefan looked suspiciously at the plate, saying, "No, I have never had oysters."

"Then you have mine!" said Mirko. "These are good and fresh, just from water today."

Stefan eyed the oysters, seeing them raw in their own juice.

Before he could say he didn't want any, Klara said, "You will insult my cousin if you don't take a taste. After all, he is treating you as a guest and not a customer."

Mirko took an oyster on the half shell in his hand saying, "Here I show you." With a fork, he loosened the oyster, put the wide end of the shell to his lips and let the oyster slip into his mouth. After he swallowed he said, "See, it is good for you."

Klara was enjoying this. She said to Stefan, "You must eat four." Seeing his surprised look, she said with a wicked smile, "It is known that raw oysters make a man very good in bed."

Stefan looked at Klara seeing she was enjoying herself seeing his discomfort. He picked up an oyster and loosened it with his fork. Before he put the shell to his lips he said, "You are wasting these on me. There won't be a woman in my bed tonight."

It didn't take long for the fishermen in Mirko's place to accept Stefan. Some were friendlier than others, stopping to introduce themselves and shake hands.

Klara smiled watching Stefan, pleased that he was so kind to all who came to speak with him.

Klara announced that it was time for her to home. Stefan left with her and walked on the road paved with crushed sea shells. The two new friends walked feeling comfortable together. Stefan had his suit coat draped over one shoulder.

Stefan stopped walking, leaning against a waist high stone wall. Klara stood next to him, watching as he took his cigarette case from his pocket. Before taking one, he offered the open case to Klara. She lifted one out, hearing him say, "Take another."

The two friends leaned against the wall smoking their cigarettes enjoying being together.

Stefan said, "You were right about what you saw in my coffee cup. I met a woman from my past today. You said I would need strength to face the future. What this woman said to me is changing how I wanted to live."

Klara turned towards Stefan. Seeing her solemn face disturbed him. He asked, "What is the matter? I said you were right. The reading of the coffee cup grounds came true."

"Give me your right hand." she said.

He switched his cigarette to his left hand, finding her fortune telling amusing, he smiled at her. She looked at his open palm for what seemed to Stefan a long time. He was about to ask her what was taking so long, when she said, "Stefan...the future I was seeing has not arrived yet. Neither has the woman who will change your life and how you will live."

Stefan said, "I already saw the woman who has changed the way I wanted to live." He was referring to Barbra.

Klara said nothing more, just shrugged her shoulders.

Stefan wanted to ask Klara more, when he saw two older women all in black. There heads were covered with black babushkas...scarves tied under their chins. He looked back and saw they had come through a walkway in the stone wall. Behind the wall, for the first time, he noticed a church with a small cemetery at one side.

Klara nodded to the women, saying "Dobar dan...Good day."

The women, not stopping, murmured the same to Klara, looking sideways at the handsome stranger.

Klara indicated with a nod of her head, "That is our church, Sveti Nikola...Saint Nicholas." She let out a low laugh, "Members of this church want to change the name to Sveti Andra...St. Andrew, but it has been Nikola for so very long. Every once in a while, people will argue about it, since Andra is the saint of fishermen." She shrugged her shoulders, "This church was here long before most of us arrived."

Stefan dropped his cigarette and stepped on it. He said, "I want to go in the church."

Klara said, "Go ahead. It is always open. I have to hurry home." As she started to walk away, she said, "I'll be working tomorrow. Come and see me. Tomorrow I will be making grah i zele...beans and sauerkraut."

Stefan watched Klara walk away for a while before going into the churchyard. Here, he saw the same stone or cement burial tombs he saw in the city.

There were wooden, double church doors with huge ornate brass hinges. Stefan pulled on the curved brass door handle. Once inside, Stefan saw the marble holy water font in the entrance. He dipped his fingers in the water then made the sign of the cross as he genuflected.

As he looked around the church, smelling of flowers, melting wax, and incense, he realized he was alone.

The church was so quiet that Stefan heard the sound of his shoes hitting the floor as he walked to the very first pew in front of the altar. Above the low wooden altar hung a large wooden hand carved crucifix of Christ.

He knelt on the kneeler, closing his eyes. He breathed in the scent of the burning candles. Stefan felt as if he had been transported to his father's chapel on Vladezemla, the chapel which had been behind the house on the far side of the kitchen garden.

With his eyes closed, in his mind he was again young and praying for forgiveness for so many youthful transgressions. *Is that was he wanted to do here?*

He remembered stealing his mother's treasured earrings to pay off a gambling debt. Also the memory of his dislike of Katya because his aunt no longer doted on him, but planned to leave everything to Katya, the daughter she thought was dead. He remembered also...leaving his Barbra alone in Zagreb while he and Ignatz came to America.

He didn't know how long he knelt there or how long he was lost in his thoughts. When he opened his eyes, the church was no longer dimly lit, but a bright shaft of sunlight blazed through the stained glass windows bringing the interior of the church alive. Colors played on the white altar cloths while bathing the statues in bright colors.

Stefan saw a side table with candles before the statue of the Blessed Virgin. At home in his father's chapel, there was a pan of earth from the garden. When Stefan lit a candle, he would set it upright in the soil. Here he saw beautiful red glass candle holders. Each was filled with white wax.

Stefan still not wearing his suit coat, reached into an inside pocket. He took out a smooth leather money folder where he drew out a five dollar silver certificate. He folded the money into a size that would fit into the coin slot below the candles.

He did not kneel and pray after having lit any candles. Looking at the statue of Mother Mary, he felt she knew what he wanted. The first two candles he lit were for his two lost babies, then for his father, and another for his mother. Lastly, he just lit all the candles that were in one row.

He stepped away from the candle stand going to the rail in front of the altar. There he made the sign of the cross while he genuflected.

He and his American wife, Adele, went to the Presbyterian Church, but he never felt it was right for him. Here in Sveti Andra, he was at home.

Out in the churchyard, he felt content. It was as though the last two years in Chicago no longer mattered to him. He thought of Barbra, but not with the same pain and anger he had felt earlier.

As he left the churchyard, walking on the road of crushed shells, he felt that New Orleans was a beginning for him. He had felt it in the church. Now was the time for him to let go of the past. Maybe Klara's reading of the coffee grounds would come true. Just maybe he needed his strength for the future. Klara had said that a woman would change the way he would live, but at this time, he wasn't thinking of women. He was thinking of what New Orleans had to offer him.

CHAPTER 14

Stefan, with his suit coat loose over his shoulders, walked along the waterfront having left the church. He didn't stop at any of the cafés nor did he stop to talk with the people he passed, though he would nod a greeting.

He lost track of time while walking, no longer recognizing anything. Stefan found himself in an area of the river where there were many boats. Just a few were fishing vessels. One large boat caught his eye. It was a huge steam-driven paddleboat. He had never seen one before, but remembered hearing about these boats.

Sitting on a stone wall, he lit a cigarette and watched the activity taking place on these boats. It didn't take him long to realize the boats were in various stages of repair. His eyes kept returning to the large paddleboat which had several decks. These boats usually had a name painted on the hull, but this one had been scraped, so that Stefan could only make out what he thought to be the letter R.

He found that the activity on this boat interested him. Stefan caught the attention of a workman carrying some lumber on his shoulder. He asked the man, "What are you doing on that boat?"

The tanned, burly workman was glad for a reason to stop and catch his breath. He set down the lumber and looked up, just as Stefan held open his cigarette case to the man. A bit surprised at the friendly gesture from such a nicely-dressed man, he nodded, taking a cigarette.

Once the cigarette was lit and the man took a puff, he said, "We are getting it ready for the owner to sell. He wants it in perfect condition so he can get the best price for it."

Stefan studied the boat with narrowed eyes, he asked, "Why is he selling it? Is competition so great he isn't making any profit?"

"Oh, no." said the man, now leaning on the wall next to Stefan, finding he felt very comfortable with this stranger. "The owner's wife died and he wants to go to California to be with his brother. I think his brother has a hotel there."

"Do you think I could go on the boat and look around?" asked Stefan.

"I can ask. By the way, I am Joe." He said as he lifted the wood and balanced it again on his shoulder. "Thanks for the cigarette." He adjusted his cap over a head of curly, brown hair, paused a moment before leaving. "Wait here and I will ask our boss if you can come aboard."

While Stefan waited for Joe to return, he watched the activity that was happening on the boat. There was some pulling out of old wood and the sound of hammers pounding nails on new replacement wood.

Not knowing anything about boats, Stefan was nevertheless impressed by the size of this one. It appeared large to him. He counted four levels, the very top with only a square cabin perhaps for the captain of the boat. The first, lowest level had fencing around it, possibly for cargo. The second and third levels had many doors and a safety rail all along the side of the boat.

From where he leaned against the stone wall, Stefan could see his new friend, the laborer, Joe, on the first level of the boat talking with someone. The person he was talking to looked in Stefan's direction. There was more talk between the two men. It appeared that Joe was doing some convincing, because it took a while before Joe came off the boat to where Stefan waited.

Joe, his shirt damp from sweat, said to Stefan, "My boss was afraid to let you on the boat, but I convinced him that you could be interested in buying it." Then he added, "If he could tell the owner that he helped sell the boat, it would maybe make him look good to the owner."

Stefan picked up his jacket from where it was placed on the wall. He walked with Joe, aware that many curious eyes, on the dock and on the boat, followed them.

Stefan and Joe walked across a shaky wooden walkway from the dock onto the boat where tanned, tough-looking man waited for them. The man's eyes studied Stefan as Joe said, "This is the boss of the repair crew."

Stefan put out his hand saying, "Thanks for letting me look around. I am Stefan Vladeslav."

"I am Paulo." said the man in charge. He noticed the gold ring with the crest when he shook hands with Stefan. The ring impressed him. Now he was not so reluctant to let Stefan look around the boat.

Just as Paulo was about to take Stefan around, a large, horse-drawn wagon with barrels of supplies, wood, and drums of paint came into sight.

"Shit!" said Paulo, seeing the wagon. This meant he would not be the one to show Stefan the boat as he was sure Stefan was someone very important.

Before Paulo could make a decision, Joe said to his boss, "Go ahead. I can show him the boat."

Paulo was annoyed, but knew he needed to see what was in the wagon and make sure nothing had been shorted.

Joe stepped back to let Stefan go before him.

"What is all this fencing?" asked Stefan, as the started to walk on the first deck.

"This is where we load the cargo." said Joe. Some of it is bales of cotton, maybe bananas, silk cloth from Europe, and even some animals would be in the back. Along this part of the deck we pile up wood for steam. Often we have to pick up more wood along the way to St. Louis."

Joe led Stefan up a staircase to the second level. "Here we serve food and occasionally there is entertainment."

On the third deck, Stefan and Joe walked seeing rows of doors that opened out onto the deck. Stefan pulled one door open looking in. He saw a small room with bunks for sleeping. These particular cabins were very plain. What Stefan had seen on the trains appeared more inviting than these.

Stefan said, "These rooms don't look very comfortable."

Joe said, as he led Stefan around the outer deck, "This boat is one of the older ones. I have seen the newer ones and they are really something. That is why we are here to make this old steamboat a showplace."

Stefan and Joe walked around the boat for almost half an hour. Joe didn't ask any questions, but looked at Stefan's face often to see if he could read his thoughts.

When they were down on the lower deck, Stefan shook Joe's hand. "Thanks for showing me around and explaining things to me. How long do you think it take for this crew of men to finish the work?"

"I'm guessing it will take a while." Joe said, leaning against a railing, "This is an old boat. It will take a lot of time and work to make it look like the newer Mississippi steamboats."

"Thanks, Joe. I'll be seeing you again."

Stefan didn't see the crew boss as he walked over the wooden planks to get to the pier. He walked a while, stopping to look back at the old boat. He wasn't sure why he was drawn to the boat. He knew nothing about boats.

Could he make money with that boat? Could he live on the boat?

Walking away from the docks along a street lined with trees, Stefan hailed a carriage. He didn't know the name of the street where the Dalmatcia hotel was located. It didn't matter, the coachman knew.

On the ride to the Dalmatcia, once again traffic was stopped because of a funeral parade. This time Stefan didn't get out of the carriage as he had gotten off the streetcar the first time he saw such a parade.

The coachman of this carriage was Black, so Stefan said, "I am not from these parts. So I don't understand all this happiness at a funeral."

The coachman, a very handsome, tall man, dressed in a long black coat and a black top hat said, "It goes back to the slave days. Back then, I am told, that when a baby was born, the women in the family would cry because they gave birth to a slave, a slave who would have a terrible life." He looked at Stefan for a reaction, not seeing any he continued, "When the slave died, it meant his life of terrible pain was over, so there was rejoicing."

"Is that true?" asked Stefan.

The coachmen looked away from Stefan to the parade, now disappearing down the street, allowing traffic to continue. He said, "Well, that's what the old women say."

CHAPTER 15

In Stevo's office at the hotel, he and Brouchard were pouring over the Chicago newspaper pages sent to them by Coralynn. Both Stevo and the banker were delighted looking at the full pages of pictures of Michael DuKane and his artworks. There were also pictures of Coralynn modeling various dresses sold by Marshall Fields.

The pictures and interviews of both Michael and Coralynn delighted Brouchard. He was especially impressed with the comments made by the well-known French photographer, Edda, about Michael's paintings.

Harold Brouchard cut the end of his cigar while Stevo filled two glasses with the Yelich wine. Harold said, "Steve, did you ever think when Coralynn and Michael got married, that it would turn out so well for them. I mean, look at them!" He pointed to various pictures of Coralynn, saying, "I have known her since she was born and I tell you, her smiles in those pictures are genuine."

Stevo also smiled, looking at a photograph of Michael against a wall pointing to his painting of a stunning woman with honey-colored hair. He said, "We can hope that anyone who sees that particular picture has never been to New Orleans or to the House of the Rising Sun."

At that, Harold burst out laughing. He said, "I remember how upset you were when the girl was modeling in his studio. You were hoping none of the hotel guests recognized her or connected her with the Dalmatcia."

He puffed on his cigar. Still laughing, he said, "Men might have thought our hotel was offering a different kind of service."

There was a knock on the office door.

"Yes?' said Stevo. Louis, the desk clerk, said, "Mr. Vladeslav wishes to speak with you."

The banker started to rise from his chair not wanting to see Stefan. Stevo motioned for Harold to remain seated, saying, "Let's hear what he wants now that Barbra let him know she didn't want him."

Louis held open the door as Stefan entered. Neither Stevo nor Brouchard stood to greet him. There was an awkward moment when Stefan saw the banker in the room. He said, "I am sorry. Am I interrupting something?"

Stevo said, "Pull a chair to the desk and tell us why you are here."

When Stefan reached for the chair, he noticed the painting of Katya, the same one he saw in Marshall Fields. He said, "I saw a copy of that painting in Chicago."

"Yes, it is a copy."

It was now close to six o'clock. Stevo wanted to go home to Barbra, Brouchard wanted some dinner then to go to his room in the hotel. Stefan was excited and wanted to talk about the paddleboat.

"What can we do for you?" asked Stevo.

Stefan leaned forward in his straight-backed chair. He said, "I want to stay in New Orleans."

Both Brouchard and Stevo were taken aback by this announcement. The banker looked at Stevo, wondering what he was going to say. Stevo stared at Stefan for what seemed a long time. At last, he said, "Why would you want to stay? Barbra has made it clear that she is not going back to you."

Stefan had pushed Barbra out of his mind for most of the day. What Stevo said gave him a small jolt, but not one that would keep him of asking what he needed to know. Dismissing the comment, Stefan said, "I find that I like New Orleans. It has such a European feel to it." He pulled out his cigarette case offering it to Stevo, who shook his head, pointing to his own pack of Camels on the desk. Brouchard had a cigar in his hand.

The two men waited while Stefan lit his own cigarette, then, he said, "Chicago has none of the charm of New Orleans. The people, the food, all excite me."

Stevo pursed his lips, let out a sigh saying to Stefan, "I don't have to tell you that you have no friends here. A man needs friends."

Stefan looked earnestly at Stevo, and then at Brouchard. He paused before saying, "Stevo, I know I was rude when I was in Gary." He stamped out his half smoked cigarette in the desk ashtray.

"You certainly were." said Stevo. "You made us all feel as if we were not good enough for you to associate with us. And," Stevo continued, "You let me know you thought my merchandise in the store was inferior to what you were used to."

Brouchard said nothing, just looked from Stevo to Stefan, not sure why he was in the room hearing this.

Stefan leaned closer to the desk. He looked at Stevo, paused, and then said, "Look, Stevo, I had just left Barbra. I felt she had deserted me for her home in Germany with her father." He stood up, pacing in front of the desk. No one said a word, waiting for him to go on with what he had started to say.

"Look," he said again, "without Barbra my business was dying. She didn't write to me and I thought she and Josef had something going on."

"So," said Stevo, "what does this have to do with how you behaved with me?" He added, "And how you made me feel my hospitality was beneath you."

Stefan stood still, staring at Stevo, and then shifting his gaze to Brouchard, who looked without expression at him.

He collapsed in the chair and buried his face in the palms of his hands, his elbows on the desk.

Brouchard and Stevo, not saying anything, exchanged questioning looks.

It seemed a very long time before Stefan dropped his hands from his face and straightened up in his chair.

Stefan said, "I have changed. I am not the same person who was at your store in Gary. That was when I was sad and bitter." He looked from Stevo to Brouchard, his eyes almost pleading, "Before I left Zagreb, my second unborn son had died. Barbra was gone…everything was lost to me."

Brouchard relit his cigar, which had gone out. While he puffed on the cigar, he studied Stefan. After a while, he said, "You want us to be your friends, is that it?"

Stefan's face brightened at the hope of friendship. He said, "Yes, I would like us to be friends, but I want more."

Stevo and Brouchard again exchanged questioning looks.

Before Stevo could say anything, Brouchard said, "I only met you a day ago. What Bobo told me left me not wanting to have anything more to do with you. I am too old to deal with dishonorable people. How do Steve and I know that you are not going to use us in some dishonest way?"

Stefan stood up and again nervously paced the small area in front of the desk. He stopped in front of the banker saying, "You know what my assets are. You have them in your bank. What I would like is your opinion on what I am thinking of doing and who you trust to help me."

Stevo said, "Before we make any promises, tell us what you are thinking of doing."

Now Stefan sat down, sitting sideways so that he could look across the desk at Stevo and Brouchard who was sitting alongside of him.

He was becoming excited because he felt the two men were listening and that was a good sign. Stefan said, "I was walking along the waterfront and I saw where men were working on a boat. Once it is repaired, the owner wants to sell it."

Stevo said, "You aren't a fisherman." Brouchard said, "Fishing is a hard life. Most of the fishermen here were born to it."

Stefan was smiling as he said, "No, not a fishing boat, a paddleboat to travel up the Mississippi."

Both Brouchard and Stevo stared open mouthed at Stefan. After some surprised silence, the older man asked, "Why do you want to do that? You know nothing about riverboats or the kind of men you need to hire."

Stefan looked from Stevo to Brouchard, he said, "I want to be part of New Orleans. I know that is what I want to do. I want to meet new people and make a new life for myself."

Stevo stood up, looking at Stefan. He said to him, "You know this new life you want in New Orleans is not going to include Barbra."

For a moment, Stefan didn't say anything. It was as though Stevo had knocked the wind out of him. He composed himself, saying, "I know Barbra is part of my past." He studied Stevo's serious look. He inhaled deeply saying, "Stevo, I will make no contact with Barbra. I know she wants to be with you. I will respect that."

Brouchard and Stevo looked at one another, as if reading each other's minds. Finally, Brouchard said to Stefan, "Let Steve and me talk about this. We need to decide just how good an idea you have and how workable it would be for you."

Smiling happily, Stefan took Brouchard's hand and shook it. He then reached across the desk to shake Stevo's hand. He said, "I know my life is about to change." Then he laughed, saying, "A woman read my fortune and said I would need strength for the change coming my way."

CHAPTER 16

When Stefan awoke the next morning, it was with a sense of contentment that he had not had since arriving in America. It was as if he knew his life was going to change and with it, his life would have a new purpose.

Still on the dresser was the portrait of Barbra. It was as though the sunlight coming through the balcony doors reached for her red hair. He knew he would not pursue Barbra…and yet…what if she changed her mind and came to him?

He was in no hurry to leave his room. After washing and shaving, he dressed in a navy blue silk robe. When he opened the double doors leading to his very small metal balcony, he decided to have his breakfast brought up to the room. A porter answered Stefan's ring immediately, taking the breakfast order.

Stefan had not fully unpacked, thinking he would not be staying at the hotel for any length of time, but now, he changed his mind. While unpacking his traveling trunk, he found the silver picture frame with the Croatian crest at the top and the Vladeslav crest at the bottom of the frame. It had been a wedding gift from Adele. She had their wedding picture in the frame when she gave it to him.

Before leaving Chicago, he had removed the picture from the frame, placing it on Adele's dressing table with his wedding ring on the picture.

Stefan sat in the chair, enjoying the soft, morning breeze along with his first cigarette and cup of coffee. He wished he had someone to take along to the dock to show off the boat he was sure he wanted to buy. He could think of no one.

Stefan ate his eggs and grits while looking out over an area of small houses. The activity on the street below was coming alive with street vendors and early shoppers.

He left his tan suit on the bed with a note for it to be pressed when the maid came in to make the bed.

Today he dressed in a lightweight brown suit with a white shirt and the cravat, as he called his brown- and white-striped tie. In Croatia he grew up referring to neckties as cravats. A tie around the neck came into fashion in the 1650s following the scarves worn by Croatians who fought with the French Army in the Thirty Years War. At that time, the Germans called Croatians Krabats which became Cravats.

In the lobby, Stefan looked about for Stevo or the older Brouchard. Not seeing either of them in the lobby, Stefan went to the dining area where, seeing Stevo, he approached the table.

As Stefan neared the table, Stevo asked, "Had your breakfast?"

Stefan replied, "Yes."

"Well then, sit and have some coffee." said Stevo, spreading some fruit marmalade on a breakfast roll.

A server appeared almost immediately. Stefan said, "Just some coffee."

Looking at Stevo, he asked, "Can I count on you and Harold Brouchard to help me with acquiring the boat?"

Stevo put down his roll while giving Stefan a serious look. He said, "We haven't decided. However, if we don't help you, we will do nothing to keep you from getting what you want." He took a sip of coffee and continued, "Harold is at the bank now, looking to see if we can determine who the owner of the boat might be."

Stefan smiled. What Stevo said gave him confidence in going forward with his plans. He said, "Thanks, Stevo. You are a much better man than I gave you credit for back in Gary." He put out his hand to Stevo, "I hope this will be the beginning of a real friendship with our past behind us."

Stevo shook Stefan's hand saying, "Our tomorrows can be better."

Leaving Stevo, Stefan stopped in the hotel gift shop where he regularly bought his Fatima cigarettes. In New Orleans, he went hatless because his felt hats from Chicago were wrong for the warm climate. He took the time to look over a row of Panama straw hats at the back of the gift shop. After trying on a couple in front of a small mirror, he decided on one which he wore leaving the shop.

Unsure of how to find the part of the river where boats were stored or being repaired, Stefan stopped a jitney, which is what the French called the cabs, because the cost was only a nickel.

His taxi ride was pleasant enough and soon Stefan saw he was on the riverfront where he wanted to be.

He walked slowly to the boat, seeing the same activity he had seen the day before. There were men hauling planks of wood on their shoulders or carrying buckets of nails.

Once again, he leaned against a low wall near where he met the burly worker, Joe, the day before. He wondered if he would be seeing Joe today.

Pleased that he had bought the hat, which shaded his eyes, he lit a cigarette to watch the progress of the boat he hoped would be his one day.

His eyes scanned the boat from top to bottom watching the workers as they moved about. He straightened himself, no longer leaning on the wall. Did he see a woman on the lower deck? It appeared she was shouting at the man Stefan met the day before who was the boss or foreman. He couldn't hear what was being said, but he could tell by the way the woman stood boldly in front of the man it appeared she was giving orders.

"You are back." Stefan recognized Joe's voice. The worker only paused for a moment saying, "Can't visit today. We barely get a chance for a drink of water."

Stefan offered his open cigarette case to the worker, whose shirt was soaked in sweat.

Joe, smiling, took a cigarette and tucked it above his ear to keep it dry. "Thanks." he said, "I'll have to smoke it later." He was gone before Stefan could ask who and why the woman on the deck was shouting so loudly that Stefan could hear her voice, but not make out the words.

Stefan watched for a while. Curious, he started to walk to the boat. As he neared, he still heard the woman's voice and occasionally the foreman replying.

Seeing the same wooden boards used as a walkway onto the boat, Stefan walked across them. Once on the first deck, he walked towards the sound of the woman's voice.

The woman was slender and rather plain. Her brown hair was tied back into a bun. Her brown eyes were narrowed and her voice was shrill as Stefan heard her say, "What do you mean you need more than a month to finish the work on this boat? Hire more men."

In a pleading voice, the frustrated man said, "I don't need more men. I need to finish certain jobs before we can go on to the next."

Stefan walked slowly toward the two, noticing the man's shirt was torn and dirty from work. The woman wore a green long skirted dress with long sleeves ruffled at the cuffs.

Noticing Stefan approaching, the woman said loudly, "Please leave the deck. You have no business here."

The foreman, seeing Stefan, said to the annoyed woman, "This is the man who may be interested in buying the boat."

With her hands on her hips and eyes shooting darts at the foreman, she said, "This boat is not for sale!"

"But, Miss Daniels, your father said he wanted the boat repaired so he could sell it."

Miss Daniels glared at the workman. "I said it is not for sale." she repeated.

The foreman turned to Stefan, visibly embarrassed. He said "I am sorry." Shaking his head he said, "I must have misunderstood."

Stefan was sure that the man had not misunderstood. He had no idea why Miss Daniels had authority concerning the boat. He decided he didn't like this woman. He preferred a woman with charm, not one who made those working for her to be humiliated.

Without a word, Stefan reached into his inside jacket pocket. He pulled out a soft leather money folder, where he also kept his calling cards.

He gave the now curious woman an exaggerated bow. He handed her his calling card, tipped his hat respectfully to the foreman as he walked off the boat never looking back.

The woman's jaw dropped as she read COUNT STEFAN VLADESLAV. There was nothing more on the card, just the title.

Stefan walked quickly, not wanting her to send someone after him.

After reading the card, her cheeks were red. "Why didn't you tell me who he was?" she whispered to the foreman in a strained voice.

The man said, "I don't know who he is. He just came yesterday and asked for a tour of the boat. Your father said he wanted to sell it, so I let this man look around."

She asked, "Any idea where he is staying?"

The man shook his head. "No. Yesterday was the first time I saw him."

Miss Daniels read the calling card out loud, "Count Stefan Vladeslav."

The foreman said, "I don't know what that means or who he is."

Her eyes searched the riverfront, but there was no sign of Stefan.

She said, "It means he is goddamned royalty!"

Miss Sara Daniels flipped Stefan's calling card back and forth in her hands. She felt the need to find out who this man Vladeslav is and what he wants with her boat. She considered it her boat, though it belonged to her father, who was still in mourning two months after his wife's passing.

Sara Daniels was in deep thought as she stared at the waterfront, thinking about the man she just met.

The foreman was becoming nervous, he had work to do. Not wanting her to start yelling at him again, he interrupted her thoughts saying, "Miss Daniels, if you are done with me, I should get back to my men."

With her eyes still searching the waterfront for Stefan, she said absently, "Yes, sure, go ahead."

As the foreman walked away, he looked back at Sara Daniels, wondering what she had in mind that made her so quiet.

Sara, deep in thought, walked slowly to the makeshift gangway.

Why would a man of such means want to buy this old boat once named, The Rose?

Sara picked up her parasol. She was one of those Southern women who wanted to keep her skin as white as possible, always shading her face with a parasol or wide-brimmed hat. As she slowly walked off the boat, named after her mother, Rose, Sara was determined to find out where she could find this Count Vladeslav.

Walking to the road, she waited only a short time for a carriage to come by. Once inside the carriage, she decided to go to the First National Bank to find out the condition of her father's finances. He would never talk money with his wife or daughter, thinking women had no mind for business.

Sara, being the only child, had always been with her father. She remembered when he bought the boat. She had sat at the bank when he borrowed money to purchase it. As a little girl, she played on the dock or on the boat while cargo was loaded and passengers came aboard.

Damn it, she thought. *I am every bit as smart as any son he could have had.*

At the bank, Sara walked directly to where Brouchard's desk was. She didn't have Harold's secretary announce her, just went right to his desk.

Looking up, surprised, Brouchard said, "Sara. How are you?" not waiting for a reply, he asked, "How is your father? Is something wrong?"

Sara took a deep breath before saying, "Mr. Brouchard, I need help."

"Sit down, Sara. What can I help you with?"

When they were both seated, Sara said, "My father thinks he wants to sell the boat. Now that Mother is gone, he doesn't want to stay in New Orleans."

Upon hearing "My father thinks he wants to sell the boat." Something clicked in Brouchard's head.

Sara asked, "I need to know about my father's finances. He never would discuss money with Mother or me, but now I need to know why he is in a hurry to sell the boat."

Of course, the old baker knew all about John Daniels' financial problems. He had worked with Sara's father for more than twenty years.

The problem with Sara's father's finances had been his desire to live a grand life. Elegant balls, garden parties, and trips to Europe for Sara, kept Daniels always strapped for money.

Wanting to stall Sara, Brouchard said, "Does your father know you are asking about his finances? I don't usually disclose this information without the primary person's permission."

Sara forced herself to remain calm. If Sara had been a son instead of a daughter, she would already have the accounts on the desk in front of her.

She said, "I am worried about my father. He sits in his study with a glass of bourbon almost every day. He doesn't talk to me or tell me what his plans are." Folding her hands on the desk, she continued speaking, "Today I found out he wants to sell the boat. He has a full crew of men working on the boat and I don't know if there is money to pay them."

Now, Brouchard was concerned. He didn't know that men had been hired to make the boat beautiful again.

He said to Sara, "I will come and see your father. He might tell me what his is thinking and what his plans are." To Sara, he said apologetically, "I know here in the South we don't burden our women with talk of money."

"Thank you, Mr. Brouchard. I think it might help if you would come to see Father." She started to rise, changing her mind, she remained seated. She took from her small purse the calling card the handsome stranger had given her.

Handing it to Brouchard, she said, "This man came to the boat today. He did not speak to me, but the foreman told me that he was there yesterday and was interested in buying the boat."

It was all Brouchard could do to not show surprise and to remain composed. Seeing the card: COUNT STEFAN VLADESLAV stunned the banker. He wondered if Steve knew that Stefan was a European count.

When Sara left, with the calling card, Brouchard called the local library. Knowing the head librarian for many years, he asked, "Hello, Alma? If I give you a name can you trace it to see if it is in any way royalty?"

CHAPTER 17

It was 1:30, past lunch time. Brouchard could not wait for the librarian to call him back. He was so surprised to discover Stefan was a count that he knew he couldn't concentrate on his work at the bank.

Bobo would not be at the bank until later in day as he always came to take Brouchard to the hotel.

Telling his secretary that something very important had to be attended to, Brouchard hurried out of the bank and hailed a passing taxi.

On the way to the Canal Street courtyard, Bobo spotted the banker in the cab. Knowing it was not like Brouchard to leave the bank until four in the afternoon, Bobo was concerned. *Could the older man be ill?* He wondered.

Bobo followed the taxi all the way to the courtyard. Brouchard exited the cab on the street and hurried in to the patio, where he hoped to find Barbra.

Bobo didn't stay. He didn't want Brouchard to think he was being spied upon. Bobo would ask Cleona later what this trip was about.

Seated at the wrought iron table, Barbra and the children were having a light lunch of mixed fruit.

Delighted to see Brouchard, Barbra gave the man a warm smile, saying, "I am so happy to see you. But, how can the bank get along without you?"

Before Brouchard could sit down, Little Kate had her arms wrapped abound her grandfather's waist. She squealed in delight. "What a surprise. Can you stay the rest of the day?"

He picked her up, realizing he was not as young and strong as he once was, and that she was growing bigger each day.

He said breathing heavily, "You aren't my Little Kate anymore. I can't pick you as easily as I used to."

Kate laughed, squirming out of his arms, as he was relieved to have her down on the ground.

Cleona heard the voices and came out from the house to the patio. Seeing Brouchard, she said, "Want something cold to drink, how about some lunch?"

He gave Cleona a warm smile. "Something cold to drink would be fine." Looking seriously at Barbra, he said, "I have to talk with Barbra."

Cleona sensing something important was about to happen, said to the children, "You come in the house with Cleona. When you finish your lunch, you can help me with the dishes."

With a pout, Little Kate said to her grandfather, "I don't want to leave. You just came."

Brouchard put his arm around Little Kate saying, "Go with Cleona. When Barbra and I have finished our talk, you can come out. I may even take you and Joso for a walk and buy you some sweets."

Clever Little Kate looked at her grandfather. She narrowed her eyes, saying, "Alright, Grandpère. I know you want to talk about something you don't think I should hear." She went into the house.

In just a minute, Little Kate appeared with a cold glass of lemonade for her grandfather. As she set the glass down, she said with a pout, "Remember, you are going to take Joso and me for some sweets when you have finished your conversation with Barbra."

Brouchard smiled, watching his adorable grandchild. She was all he had left. He had his niece Coralynn, but Kate was his and so special.

He noticed a copy of the Chicago newspaper on the table. Brouchard said, "I see you have read about our Michael and Coralynn." He leaned forward looking at the pictures remarking, "They do look happy, don't they?"

Barbra smiled saying, "Alright Harold, you didn't leave the bank to come for lemonade and to talk about the newspaper pictures."

From his vest pocket, he pulled out a cigar, broke off the end, all the while studying Barbra's face. He lit the cigar and took a couple of puffs wondering how to ask her about Stefan. He wondered if she would be offended that he wanted to question her about him.

Barbra looked lovely wearing a white lace dress with buttons down the front so she could easily nurse Gabriella, who was now asleep in her wicker carriage.

Smiling, Barbra asked, "Well, Harold. Why are you here?"

He cleared his throat, flicking an already formed ash from his cigar, "Tell me about Stefan."

Barbra's eyes widened, her lips parted in surprise. She asked, "Why do you want to know about Stefan? I am sure you already know that we were married in Zagreb."

"Something happened at the bank which finds me needing to know more about him."

Barbra straightened in her chair, leaning her elbows on the table. She said, "I know nothing about his finances. I don't see how I can be of any help."

Taking another puff on his cigar, Brouchard said slowly, and in an almost low voice, "You can tell me if he is royalty."

The stunned look on Barbra's face changed in an instant. She burst out into laughter, saying "Don't tell me you believe that?"

All at once, she became serious asking, "Were you here last summer when I told Michael I was a countess?"

Her hands were together as if in prayer up at her lips. She looked at Brouchard, her eyes wary, as if she feared something was going to happen.

Brouchard said, "A bank customer came in yesterday. She showed me Stefan's calling card. It showed in raised print, COUNT STEFAN VLADESLAV."

Barbra was speechless. She couldn't believe it. After a long silence she said, "I heard that Stefan's father could use the title of count if he wanted to, but he never did. Actually, we never talked about it or even referred to it. I think I just heard of it in some unimportant conversation."

She tapped her fingers absently on the table. She said excitedly, "I remember how it came up in conversation. Stefan's father lived with us in the apartment above the store. At lunch one day, he said how Stefan's mother would be horrified to know he lived above the store. He also said something about how unhappy she was that they live such a simple life in the country since he was a count."

Brouchard said, "I wonder why Stefan felt the need to use the title now."

Barbra's face softened as she said, "He never cared about titles. In fact, he was not fond of his mother. She let the family know that she was unhappy they were never invited to the Austrian palace for events that a count should go to."

Brouchard didn't like the faraway look that came into Barbra's eyes. He certainly didn't like what she said next. "We were so happy in Zagreb, all those evening walks in the beautiful public square."

Her eyes glistened as she said, "And the dancing to the outdoor hotel musicians."

She looked up, seeing the concerned look on Brouchard's face. It became apparent to her that her reminiscing may have sounded at though she could still be in love with Stefan.

"No, Harold, no." she said, "Don't think I miss him or want him back. In the beginning, our time together was wonderful. Those days can never come back."

Harold gave Barbra a weak smile, saying, "I promised the children a walk and some sweets."

When Harold and the children were gone, Cleona pushed the wicker carriage with the just-awakening Gabriella alongside Barbra at the table.

As Cleona handed the baby to Barbra, she asked Cleona, "Did it sound as if I still cared for Stefan?"

Cleona just shrugged her shoulders and walked back into the house.

Back at the bank, it was now close to four and closing time.

As Brouchard passed his secretary's desk, she said, "You have a message on your desk from the librarian, Miss Alma."

Brouchard said nothing, just nodded. His visit with Barbra left him troubled. He loved his Steve, the son he never had.

He dialed the library and Alma answered. She said, "I never knew the Austrian history could be so interesting."

Harold and Alma had known each other since childhood and he knew she would talk his leg off if he didn't make her come to the point.

He lied, saying, "Alma, I have people here in my office, what did you find out about the Vladeslav Family?"

"Well," she said, "I found the first record of that name back in the year 1749. Maria Theresa was Empress of Austria at that time. Here, let me read to you from the book. There was a battle in which Ljubin Vladeslav fought and was later offered the title of count and offered some land."

Harold wasn't really interested in which battle, but he listened as Alma read: "The Treaty of Aix-la-Chapelle of 1748, sometimes called the Treaty of Aachen, ended the War of the Austrian Succession, then, following a congress assembled on 24 April 1748 at the Free Imperial City of Aachen, called Aix-la-Chapelle in French, then also in English in the west of the Holy Roman Empire."

Harold was not interested in the battle, just when Vladeslav was recognized with the title of count. He interrupted Alma, saying, "I don't need to know all that."

She snapped back, "Well Harold, you are going to hear it. I spent a good deal of time researching all this for you. There isn't much more."

She continued, "The resulting treaty was signed on 18 October 1748 by Great Britain, France, and the Dutch Republic. Two implementation treaties were signed at Nice on 4 December 1748 and 21 January 1749 by Austria, Spain, Sardinia, Modena, and Genoa."

When she stopped reading, Harold said, trying not to sound annoyed, "When was Ljubin Vladeslav made a Count?"

Alma said, "It was in 1750, by Maria Theresa herself."

"Thank you, Alma." said Brouchard. "You have been most helpful."

He sat at his desk, staring into space, wondering why if Stefan and his father were not interested in titles, would Stefan now use it?

The customers were all gone and the tellers and bank associates were leaving. Through the glass window, Brouchard saw Bobo in his carriage waiting for him.

Bobo didn't ask his old friend, Brouchard, why he was at the courtyard earlier.

Brouchard was deep in thought and made no conversation with Bobo, which was not unusual. Bobo knew something was bothering his friend and hoped it was not anything serious.

In the hotel lobby, where Brouchard had a permanent room, though he had a house where his sister lived, he looked around for Stevo.

He was about to ask the desk clerk for him, when Stevo came around the desk.

Stevo said, "Hello Harold," Seeing the serious look on the banker's face he asked concerned, "Is anything wrong?"

Brouchard said, "Let's sit and talk."

The two found comfortable chairs in the lobby, facing each other.

Almost immediately, Brouchard said, "I have a long-time banking customer, whose daughter came in today. She is the daughter of the man that has the boat Stefan thinks he wants to buy."

"So? What is the problem?' asked Stevo.

Brouchard shook his head slowly as if undecided what to say. Finally he said, "I don't know what to think. Stefan gave this young lady a calling card which read, Count Stefan Vladeslav."

Stevo almost laughed, but the serious look on Brouchard's face stopped him. Before Stevo could say anything, Brouchard said, "Well, he is a count. I had the librarian look up the history of the Vladeslav name and the title goes back to 1750."

Stevo said, "I thought Barbra was joking last year when she said she was a countess. It meant nothing to her. My Katya never mentioned that her uncle was a count." Stevo paused, when Brouchard said nothing, Stevo asked, "Why does this concern you?"

"I don't know. Why is he now using a title when he never has before?" said Brouchard.

Stevo said, "I don't see why it is important, but I'll see what I can find out."

Stevo said goodbye to Brouchard and went out into the road to head for Canal Street. Something made him stop and look across the way to Little Zagreb. He waited for traffic to clear before going to the entrance of Tomo's place.

As soon as Stevo entered the café, he saw Stefan, who was now at his favorite table, the one where Klara worked.

Stevo went directly to the table. Without waiting to be invited he sat down opposite a somewhat surprised Stefan, who said, "Well, good afternoon. What can I order for you?"

"Nothing." answered Stevo, "I'm here because Brouchard wants to know about your title."

Klara appeared with a plate of sauerkraut and beans for Stefan which she placed before him. Stevo shook his head indicating he wanted nothing.

Stefan, confused, looked at Stevo. Then it dawned on him what the banker must have meant. He said, "My calling card...right? It had to be the card I gave the rude woman on the boat."

"I don't care about your title, but it disturbs Harold. He wonders why you, according to Barbra, never used the title until now."

Stefan, smiling, shook his head. He said, "I gave that card to Sara Daniels because she was rude, and yes, I did it to show her she was just an ordinary person."

He picked up his fork saying, "I know it was somewhat pompous of me, but I really didn't like the woman."

"So," asked Stevo, "does this mean you are going to use the title to impress people to make them think you deserve special treatment?"

Stefan put his fork down and leaned forward saying, "God no!"

He pushed his plate of food aside, saying, "Back in Gary, I only brought up the title to Adele because I couldn't stand listening to the men in her circle of friends, saying how dumb the workers in the mill were. How if they had an accident, the mills would get behind in production."

Klara, walking past the table, saw that Stefan was not eating. Like a mother, she stopped to give Stefan a stern look and pushed the plate closer to him.

Stefan smiled, saying, "She is just like the housekeeper we had at the house when I was growing up."

He took a bite of the food, saying, "It hurt me to hear these wealthy men, not just the mill executives, but the foremen and even the bankers think our people were no more than dumb cattle."

Stefan chewed and swallowed. He said, "One night, after I spent a most disgusting evening in the Gary Hotel listening to how stupid, "those dumb hunkies were", I had all I could take. That night in our Gary apartment, I drew from memory the family crest."

Klara was back at the table staring at Stefan. Like a naughty child, he took another fork full of sauerkraut to please her.

"You should have seen Adele when I told you I had the title of count. She was beside herself with happiness. She was a countess, and she was going to let everyone know it. Her attitude towards me became one of awe. She had calling cards with my title printed, had the title of Countess Adele Vladeslav printed on her stationary, and even went to Peacock Jewelers in Chicago to have this ring with the family crest made for me." He held his hand out for Stevo to see.

When Stevo said nothing, Stefan went on. "When we were first married, I knew that some of her friends looked down on me, thinking I was after her money." He thought a moment saying, "That may have been partly true because it gave me the life I thought I wanted in America."

Stefan poured some wine into his glass, offering some to Stevo, who declined. After he took a sip of the wine, he said, "The invitations, the balls, the dinner parties appeared almost daily."

"But…but," his throat closed for a moment, "but, I was still not accepted as one of them. It was the title! It was mentioned on the society page of the paper that the Count and Countess Vladeslav appeared here or there. That was when I started to dislike Adele and the life I had chosen in America. My desire to come back to our Croatian people grew stronger each day. That is why I like this place so much."

Music was playing as Stevo left. He looked back at the table where Stefan was laughing at something the cook, Klara, was saying to him.

CHAPTER 18

The next morning, after stopping in at the bank to take care of some paperwork, Brouchard had Bobo take him to the lovely old Garden District of New Orleans. Here the oak trees shaded the walkways along the streets, leading to the impressive Victorian mansions.

Brouchard called before leaving the bank to have Sara Daniels tell her father that he was on his way.

It wasn't yet noon when the banker told Bobo to wait for him while he spoke with Mr. Daniels.

Sara Daniels, wearing a simple light peach-colored dress, answered the door. Brouchard found this unusual, as the Daniels always had live-in servants and the lady of the house never answered the door.

"I'll take your hat." said Sara, "Papa is in his study. I told him you were coming."

Brouchard had been to the Daniels house many times in the twenty-some years they knew each other. This was the first time Brouchard was there to discuss finances. In the past, business was always done at the bank.

Brouchard was surprised to see how thin John Daniels had become since the death of his wife two months ago.

John Daniels was seated in a leather Stickley Morris chair. It was the kind of chair men preferred while women sat in tiny French chairs covered with embroidered fabric.

Mr. Daniels looked pale. His face had no color. His eyes were watery under bushy, white eyebrows. His white hair was no longer nicely trimmed, but long and thin.

"Sit down, Harold." he said. "What can I offer you?" He was still in his slippers wearing a faded blue morning robe.

Sara was at the sitting room door.

Daniels asked again, "What would you like? Coffee or maybe you would rather have some bourbon?" He raised his own glass of bourbon to Brouchard.

Brouchard saw the concerned look on Sara's face. He looked at John thinking the man looked ill.

"If you have coffee made," he said to Sara, "I would like that very much."

When Sara left the room, her father looked at Brouchard with no longer a cordial look, asking, "Alright, Harold, out with it. What is this early visit about?"

Brouchard, sitting in a comfortable padded armchair, studied John Daniels. This was a different John Daniels from the gracious and generous host of the past. Now Brouchard saw an old, angry man.

"I think there is a man who might be interested in buying your boat." said Brouchard.

Daniels' face brightened. He started to reply, but stopped when Sara came into the room with the coffee, placing it on a table beside Brouchard. She went to a nearby straight-backed chair and sat down.

Her father frowned seeing her seated. He said, "Sara, dear, you must have other things to do. Our talk would bore a young woman."

"No, Papa." she said, "I have always enjoyed being with you when you did business. I was always with you while I was growing up. I understand what is said when men discuss business."

Her father's face showed some color, indicating he was becoming agitated. He said, "I would prefer that Harold and I talk privately."

Sara stood up facing her father, saying in a low, not quite angry voice, "Why Papa, because I am not a boy? Because women are just pretty ornaments without the brains to understand about finances?"

Her father was now red faced and visibly shaken by Sara's outburst. He shouted, "You leave this room this instant. How dare you speak to me in this unladylike manner in front of my guest."

Sara was angry. She gave her father a hard look before she glanced at Brouchard. With a loud slam of the door, she was out of the room.

Brouchard saw that John Daniels' hand trembled as he took a drink of bourbon from his glass. He said, "I must apologize for Sara's behavior. I allowed her to accompany me wherever I went when she was growing up." He took another sip of bourbon, "Now she thinks she knows as much about business as I do."

Brouchard picked up the cup and saucer, took a sip of the coffee and gave John Daniels a very serious look. After a pause he said, "John, does Sara know you have nothing left?"

Sara ran quickly to the terrace at the side of the house to the open window of the sitting room. She had sat and listened beneath this window many times, as a child, when her parents didn't want her to hear their conversations.

John looked at his banker and old friend, saying, "She may suspect something. You notice we no longer have servants. Sara does what she can, but the house is too large for her to take care of. She does make meals for me, but she wasn't brought up that way. Oh, God!" he said, "I never thought I would degrade myself and my daughter this way."

Brouchard said, in a very calm tone, as he opened up a folder of papers. "Let's see what we can do. Let's start with the boat. Why are you having it remodeled?"

Daniels took a deep breath, leaned back, resting his hands on the paddle arms of the Morris chair. He said, "I need to sell the boat. Fixed up it will bring more money."

Brouchard asked, "How will you pay the workers?"

"I will borrow against the house." replied the sad-looking man.

Brouchard pulled out a sheet of paper from the folder. He held it out to Daniels, saying, "You borrowed against the house when you gave the birthday ball for Sara. That was four years ago and it still has not been repaid."

"Well," said Daniels nervously, "there is Rose's life insurance. It should be coming any day now."

Brouchard said, "You cashed in the policy a year ago."

Daniels said nothing, just stared at Brouchard, who asked, "Hasn't your accountant told you all this?"

Daniels emptied his glass in one swallow. He said, "I haven't had an accountant for the last two years. He kept telling me how much I didn't have, instead of how much I was worth. DAMN IT, Harold, you know how we lived. That money came from my assets! Where are they now?"

With a heavy heart, Brouchard said, "John, you have no assets."

John shouted at Brouchard, "Then loan me some money until I can get on my feet again."

Brouchard stood up, gathering his folder of papers. With great sadness, he said, "John, the kind of money you need," he paused, then continued, "You don't have enough collateral."

John Daniels stood up on shaky legs, "Get the hell out of here! You are like all money lenders you just want to make interest off of us! Sure, when I don't need it, you give it to me, but now..." his voice cracked, "now when I could use your help...you turn your back on me."

Brouchard felt almost ill. It hurt him to see a once vital businessman who contributed to the charm of New Orleans so beaten down.

"Goodbye, John." said Brouchard, his hand on the door handle. He stood there a moment. There was nothing more he could say to John Daniels who had collapsed in his chair, not seeing, but staring out the window. Again, Brouchard said, "Goodbye, John."

Sara, outside, sitting on the cool patio bricks, had heard it all. She felt a combination of fear for what the future will bring and anger at her father who had managed to lose all of her mother's inheritance, along with his inheritance, and now, his business.

She rose slowly, wondering what she could do. She wanted to, no, she needed to get her hands on her father's accounting books. Perhaps she could make some sense of them. Hopefully, she might find a forgotten asset to bring in some money.

When she entered the sitting room, her father was refilling his glass from the almost empty bourbon bottle. She heard him say, "Shit. This is the last bottle."

He noticed Sara had entered the room. Smiling, he said, trying to sound confident, "Harold is going to help us. Just a matter of time and we will be back on our feet with everything paid off." He took a drink from the glass. Again smiling, he said, "We'll have a servant in the house and you won't have to do so much work. We will have parties again."

Sara stood in front of her seated father. He almost cringed when he saw the dark look on her face. With the sound of disgust he had never heard from his daughter, she said, "You lying fool. You drunken idiot! All this time I could have been helping you. When you let the accountant go, I could have kept your books for you. But NO! I was a woman, a Southern Belle who was only supposed to look pretty and be a wonderful hostess."

Her father seemed to grow smaller in his chair as she stood before him with her hands on hips, glaring at him.

Not knowing that her father had already sold her mother's jewelry, Sara said, "After I look over the books we will see what we can sell. We will start with mother's jewelry. Then the silver, also some of the paintings."

She turned away from him, saying, "I'm going to your den for the account books. We will start there. I'll see what I can do with the awful mess you have made of our lives."

While Sara was in her father's den, she opened drawers, searching for his account books. She did find many merchant bills stamped "OVERDUE."

At last, in a bottom desk drawer, she found the cloth-covered account books. She sat at the desk, determined to unravel the mess her father had created.

That was when she heard the gun shot!

CHAPTER 19

A few days after John Daniels' funeral, Sara Daniels, dressed in a long black-skirted dress, was sitting at Harold Brouchard's desk in the bank.

Her face was very pale, almost colorless. She had no one to turn to now that her father was gone. Sara could not sleep nights because she felt that her harsh accusing words caused her father to shoot himself.

Gone was the tough woman Sara had been. Now, she had become quiet and fearful of her unknown and penniless future. She asked Brouchard, "What do I do now?"

Brouchard usually had a lit cigar at his desk, but today, he didn't. He had been thinking about Sara and especially his last visit with her father. John Daniels had accused him of not helping a friend when needed. Of course, Brouchard could not give Sara's father any more money. He had already given the man more than he should have, according to banking rules.

With assorted documents on his desk, Brouchard had some suggestions for Sara as to her future. Hardest of all, was having to tell her that the house was no longer hers. Once news of her father's suicide became public, every person now owed money by the estate, took legal steps to collect what they could.

Sara said nothing as she looked at Brouchard. She waited for him to advise her. Gone was the confident young woman who once felt that she had a mind for business.

Brouchard felt a great sadness for the girl. He had a written plan of how he might put the finances in order. He said, "I have stopped the work on the boat. The men were not pleased, but I promised them they would be paid as soon as the estate was settled."

When Sara heard this, she said nothing.

"As for the unpaid bills, a few stores, out of respect for you and your father, cancelled the debts. But, we still have considerable bills to be paid."

Sitting with her hands folded in her lap, Sara said nothing, just looked at Brouchard with watery eyes.

"I don't see how we can save the house. There may be some money for you once it has been sold and the mortgages are paid."

This brought a reaction from Sara. She sobbed into her handkerchief saying, "Dear God, dear God."

Looking across the desk at Brouchard, she asked, "I have no one. Where will I go if I have no money?" Then she looked at Brouchard, saying, "How can I face people I have known most of my life? They will whisper about me behind my back."

Brouchard rose from his chair and went to the other side of the desk. He put his arm around Sara, saying, "We will get through this. I won't let you fight it alone. The outcome may not be what you want, but we will make it so that you can hold your head high and not be ashamed."

Sara hung onto his hand for a long time before he loosened her grip.

Back in his chair, he picked up another paper. He glanced at it and said, "We will have an auction. First, we will auction the contents of the house." Sara's eyes grew wide as Brouchard continued, "Then we will auction off the house."

She was interested. Now she asked, "And the boat? What will we do about the boat?"

Brouchard said, "That will be the last for us to deal with. There are several liens against it."

As tough as Sara had felt in the past thinking she could be a businesswoman, she now felt relieved that Brouchard was dealing with all the details.

She had done nothing, but felt very tired…tired of thinking; tired from the guilt of saying what she had said to her father before he shot himself; tired of thinking about the future, and most of all, tired of thinking about the lack of money.

Finished at the Bank, Brouchard and Sara rode in Bobo's carriage along Canal Street. The carriage pulled into the entryway to the courtyard where Barbra and the others lived.

Sara sat up straight asking, "Why are we here? What is this?"

"I once owned this house." he said, indicating the house with the patio. "Now it belongs to my friends."

As Bobo helped Sara from the carriage, Cleona came from the house going directly to Sara. She said, "Hello, Miss Sara, I'm Cleona and I will be staying with you for a few days."

Sara was confused by the activity because here was Little Kate running to her grandfather, wrapping her arms around his waist.

Laughing, he said to Sara, "This is my granddaughter, Kate."

Seeing Barbra coming from the main house with Gabriella in her arms, he said, "And this is Barbra holding baby Gabriella."

Thin Virgine appeared, holding Joso's hand.

Sara was confused and overwhelmed. She couldn't figure who Cleona was and why she had been hired as a maid for Sara.

As Cleona came to the carriage, putting her small travel bag on the front seat beside Bobo, Sara said, "I can't afford a servant."

Cleona said, "Missy, I am not your servant. I am no one's servant. Mr. Harold asked me to spend a few days with you and that is what I will be doin."

Sara looked from Cleona to Brouchard. She didn't know that to say.

Cleona gave Little Kate and Joso a kiss. She told Barbra, "I'll be back as soon as I can." Cleona climbed into the front seat of the carriage next to her cousin, Bobo. She didn't want to leave the courtyard to watch over a young woman she didn't know, but if that was what Mr. Harold wanted, she would do it.

There was no conversation on the way to the Garden District where the Daniels' house is located.

Sara was surprised to see four men waiting in the stone walkway leading to the back of the house. She turned to Brouchard, "Who are they? What are they doing here?"

The banker waived to the men, saying to Sara, "They are from the auction company here to take an inventory and start working on the publicity for the auction."

Sara looked both confused and sick. Events were moving too quickly.

Brouchard was out of the carriage, his hand outstretched to help Sara down. She sat as if frozen. *So soon?* She thought. *It is too soon to get me out of my home.*

Sara stepped out of the carriage. She avoided looking at the men from the auction house. She followed Brouchard, who had the keys to the door. He unlocked it and stepped aside to let Sara and Cleona in. She heard the men close behind coming into the house. She didn't want to talk to them. She didn't want to hear what they had to say about the things in the house. She went to her bedroom with Cleona close behind.

Saying nothing, Sara sat in an overstuffed chair next to the window.

Cleona looked around seeing a comfortable room with a large window. The room was decorated in yellow and green. The bed had a large yellow floral canopy. There was a small dressing table and a chifferobe for her clothes and shoes. These were all the furnishings in this small room.

Cleona asked, "Would you like me to get some coffee or tea for you?"

It was as though Sara had not heard Cleona, so lost was she in her thoughts. She didn't like these strange men with their pads of paper going through her house.

Cleona walked through the lovely, large home looking for the kitchen. When she found the bright, white kitchen with a wood stove, she proceeded to make a fire for the tea.

For three days, Cleona looked over Sara, who barely spoke. Cleona tried being friendly, thinking if Sara would talk, the young woman might start to feel better. Cleona gave up trying to make Sara a friend.

Cleona was worried that Sara in her despondency might try to harm herself. This thought made Cleona more watchful.

On the fourth day of Cleona's stay, Brouchard came for Sara and Cleona, to take them to the courtyard to spend the day with Barbra and the children. Brouchard felt it would be better to get Sara out of the house before people started going through the house for the pre-auction inspection.

Now in the lovely courtyard, seated at the ornate metal table in the patio, Sara looked around seeing the warm and friendly faces of Barbra, Little Kate, and the boy, Joso, all happy to have Cleona back with them.

Little Kate tried to carry Cleona's overnight bag into the house.

"Leave it be, my Kate." said Cleona. "Come here and let me see if you have grown any while I was gone."

Kate gave a disgusted look before saying, "You haven't been gone long enough for me grow any taller."

Barbra reached across the table, touching Sara's hand, saying, "I am so happy to have you here. I don't have that many visitors, especially women."

Sara looked up at Barbra. The sound of Barbra's voice and the tone of sincerity comforted Sara in a way that Cleona had not been able to do.

To Sara, Barbra said, "Here comes Virgine with some beignets and our morning coffee. To Virgine, she said, "Virgine, this is Miss Sara, a friend of Mr. Harold's. She will be spending the day with us."

Slender, light-skinned Virgine gave Sara a warm smile. "It sure is nice to meet you, Miss Sara. We don't have enough women friends here. Hope you do come more often."

Cleona, seeing Sara appear to relax, herded Kate and Joso into the house on the pretext that they needed to help her unpack.

Sara picked up the coffee cup, taking a sip. She turned her head, looking about the large courtyard seeing butterflies flitting over the lantana flowers near the white jasmine bushes.

The large carriage house at the back of the yard caught her attention.

Barbra said, "That is where Bobo lives. He keeps the horse and carriage in the barn below. Across from us, is where we live. Steve Markovich, Kate, Joso, and I, along with Virgine. And here," she turned indicating the house behind the patio, "is where Cleona now lives."

Here, with Barbra, Sara felt more relaxed. Having Cleona in her home and the men rearranging the furniture, preparing for the auction, made her uneasy, even frightened more than a little.

Barbra pushed the plate of beignets closer to Sara, who took one.

After sipping her coffee, Barbra said, "Harold told me of your troubles. When I say that I think I know what you feel, I really do."

Sara looked at Barbra. Her eyes showed interest in what Barbra was saying.

Barbra continued, "You see, we had a fine store in Europe. We sold jewelry, paintings, and antiques. I won't go into details, but when we came to America, we were almost penniless. But, with the help of friends, and Cleona was one of them, we made a new life for ourselves."

Sara looked at Barbra, thinking about what Barbra had told her. She said, "But I have no friends."

"Of course you do!" said Barbra emphatically. "You have Harold, Cleona, and now me. Later you will meet Steve at the Dalmatcia Hotel, Tom at the Little Zagreb, oh, and Ignatz, who was with us at our store in Europe."

While Barbra made Sara feel comfortable and not so alone, Brouchard was at the Dalmatcia. He found both Stevo and Stefan at the usual front table of the outdoor restaurant.

Seeing them together, he said, "Good! I want to talk to both of you."

He turned to Stefan. "I have been too busy to tell you that the owner of the boat you want to buy has shot himself, but then you may have seen it in the paper. He left his daughter penniless."

Ignoring the surprised look of the two men, Brouchard continued, "We are having an auction at the house today to raise money to pay off the debts. Even with the sale of the house, there won't be enough money to settle all the debts."

Now, he turned to Stevo. "Steve, the girl has nowhere to go. No relatives and no money. Can we set her up in one of the storage rooms near the kitchen?"

"Of course." said Stevo, "I'll have the room cleaned up and I'll have a bed put in there."

Brouchard was in a hurry to get to the auction. He said, "Thanks, Steve. I am worried about the girl. She has been so despondent. Not talking to anyone. I had Cleona stay with her the past three days. Even Cleona was worried about her."

Stefan asked, "When will the boat be auctioned off?"

Standing at the table, Brouchard said, "I don't know what we will be doing about the boat. It has so many liens against it that I haven't had time to get into them all."

As he turned to leave, he said. "I have got to hurry and get Sara's clothes out of the house before the auction starts. She and Cleona didn't do any of that. I don't know what they were thinking."

Stefan stood up, placing his napkin on his chair. He said "Let me help you. You will have plenty to do with the auctioneer and his crew. I can gather up her things and bring them here while you deal with more important matters."

Surprised at the offer of help, Brouchard smiled at Stefan. He said, "It would help me. I don't know why Cleona didn't think of it."

Stevo also stood, saying to Brouchard, "You go on ahead while I get some boxes for Stefan. He can take a taxi to the house. Leave the address at the front desk."

Arriving at the house, Stefan was surprised at the line of people waiting to register for their auction number. As he passed through the crowd, he got some surly looks from people who feared some choice items had been pre-sold.

Brouchard, seeing Stefan, led him to Sara's bedroom, which had been temporarily closed with tape. Once inside, Stefan looked around, a bit surprised to find that the bossy, rude woman he encountered on the boat had a feminine side.

He could see that he didn't have enough boxes for all the clothes he saw in the chifferobe. Not wanting to go through the house among the people inspecting the items for auction, he studied the window. It had double push out windows, large enough for him to get out of the room, without going through the house.

Once outside, he hurried to the street, finding the taxi. Both he and the taxi driver came to the back of the house to Sara's bedroom window. Only Stefan went through the window back into the room. From the window, he preceded to hand several loads of clothing from the chifferobe to the driver, who carried them past people giving him annoying looks, thinking he was taking items that should have been in the auction.

With the boxes full from items from the drawers, Stefan felt he had done all he could. Handing the last box through the window to the taxi driver, Stefan handed him some money saying, "Take these to the back door of the Dalmatcia Hotel. Ask for Mr. Steve the owner. He will know what to do with them."

Stefan stepped out of the bedroom to find a sea of people going through the house, lifting items to search for maker's names. Chairs were upended to check their condition and paintings were removed from the walls to inspect for damage.

Having never been to an auction, Stefan found what he saw very interesting. Some of the items reminded him of the merchandise he and Barbra would have sold in their store in Zagreb.

On a whim, he went to the registering table and got a numbered card used for bidding.

Back at the courtyard, Sara, for the first time since the death of her father, was smiling. She had never, ever held a baby in her arms. Today, she held two-month-old Gabriella. It was an unusual sensation for her to hold a tiny baby.

"How did you come to name her Gabriella?" asked Sara, marveling at the tiny fingers with equally tiny fingernails.

Barbra, while putting her hair up in her usual Gibson Girl bun said, "There was a charity function at the Dalmatcia for the hospital. It was an elegant affair. There, I saw one of the most beautiful women I had ever seen. She had dark eyes and dark hair. I heard someone call her Gabriella."

She smiled looking at Sara holding the baby. "When I first held the baby in my arms, I said, 'Hello, my little Gabriella.'"

As the day wore on, Sara occasionally had thoughts of what was going on at her home. There were strangers going through cabinets, drawers, and all the rooms inspecting what they might bid on.

Watching the children playing with their toys or taking turns pushing the wicker carriage with the baby not fully asleep in it, often made her laugh.

Seeing Cleona and Virgine, not as servants, but accepted as family, was new to Sara. Being from the South, Colored people were still thought of only as workers.

The children had been put down for their naps. A large umbrella now shaded the table where Sara and Barbra sat. Each slowly moved a cloth fan back and forth to cool off their face and neck. Sara looked at the fan in her hand saying, 'When someone buys my dressing table today, they will find a lovely lace fan I received for my 21st birthday."

In a low, comforting voice, Barbra said, "Don't think of what has been or was. Keep thinking about what is ahead for you. Someday you may have a fan far more elegant than the one you left behind."

Barbra, who usually napped when the children did, stayed all afternoon keeping company with Sara. It pleased her that when Sara spoke, it was no longer with the sad, lifeless voice she had when she first came.

It was now late afternoon. Sara was becoming worried. What did Brouchard have planned for her, she wondered? Did he want her to spend the night in Cleona's house?

Sara was still in her typical black dress worn for mourning. Barbra had slipped into a brown dress, instead of a brightly colored one, out of respect for Sara.

Barbra said to Cleona, "I know that Bobo is with Mr. Harold, so will you please stop a carriage for Sara and me? I think she needs to meet some new people. Do you want to go to Little Zagreb with us?"

Shocking Sara, Cleona said, "If I go there, I will climb those stairs lookin' to see if there is any lady's underwear there!"

Barbra laughed seeing the stunned look on Sara's face. She said, "Cleona has known Tom since he was a fifteen year old. She has been giving him the devil ever since he came from Europe. It has become a game he plays with her. If I were to call him now and tell him she was coming by, he would find something naughty to have on display just to hear her give him a piece of her mind."

Cleona said, "You girls go. I'm goin' to spend time with my three babies," meaning Kate, Joso and Gabriella.

It was a pleasant carriage ride in the oncoming cool evening breeze. The pace of the people on the streets was slowing, while one could still hear a street musician or a singer. Ladies selling flowers were always calling "Buy my pretty flowers."

Sara had never been on the street where the Little Zagreb and the Dalmatcia Hotel were. It was close to the French Market, but Sara had never seen these two buildings.

Sara looked across the street and realized that the footman, the doorman, and the carriage coachmen were all dressed in the red long coats and red top hats that Bobo wore.

Tomo's jaw dropped when he saw Barbra with a young woman all in black. He never expected to see Barbra without Stevo. He hurried to them saying, "Two beautiful women in one night! How lucky can I be?"

Sara didn't know what to think. When he took them, each by the elbow saying, "You will sit at my table. That way every man in the room will be jealous of me."

As they were seated at Tomo's table, Ignatz, with his face beaming with pleasure, came to the table, kissing Barbra on both cheeks.

Laughing, Barbra said to both Tomo and Ignatz, "This is my new friend Sara and I hope she will be yours."

To Sara, she said, "This is Tom, the owner of Little Zagreb and according to Cleona, the notorious man who lives upstairs." She pointed to the spiral staircase.

Barbra took Ignatza's hand, saying affectionately, "This is my dear friend Ignatz. We have been through so much together, here and in Zagreb."

Smiling, Ignatz took Sara's hand. "I am so pleased to meet you."

Seeing Sara all in black, Tomo sensed that Barbra brought her to the Zagreb to cheer her up. He, too, took her hand saying, "It is always a pleasure to meet a special friend of Barbra's. You must be special," he added, "because you are the first pretty woman she has brought here."

Sara had always thought of herself as a plain woman. But with all the compliments and the attention, her face glowed as it had never before.

The music that Sara heard and the language that was spoken were new to her. Ignatz brought a plate of cheese strudel and glasses for the wine that was already on the table.

Tomo was busy moving around the room speaking to everyone as he always did. He glanced at the table every now and then, needing to explain to those who wanted to know who the lady in black was.

Polite people passing the table would smile or bow their heads out of respect to the lady in black. No one here thought it was disrespectful of her to be out in public while in mourning.

Barbra was pleased to occasionally see Sara tap her fingers on the table in time to the music. There were times when Barbra thought she saw a bit of a sparkle in Sara's eyes.

Time passed quickly, becoming evening before the two woman realized it.

Both Barbra and Sara were surprised to find Brouchard standing at their table. He said, raising his voice to be heard over the music and the singing, "I never would have found you if Cleona hadn't told me where you were."

Sara once again became herself. The party was over. Where would she go now? Where would she live, or for that matter, where would she sleep?

"Come on, you two gadabouts." said Brouchard. To Barbra he said, with a wink, "I am taking you to Steve. He needs to know where you go when he thinks you are home with the children."

People Sara didn't know and would probably never see again waived and called their goodbyes to her.

Brouchard had Barbra by the arm on one side and Sara on the other. The smiling doorman at the hotel opened the door. This was the first time Brouchard entered the hotel with even one woman...and now there were two!

Sara's eyes widened as she saw the elegant lobby of the hotel. She wasn't sure why they were here.

Stevo was at the front desk, giving Barbra a mock, 'what are you doing here?' look.

Barbra let go of Brouchard's arm. She hurried to Stevo giving him a kiss on the cheek.

Again, Sara was surprised. She hadn't put together that Stevo and Barbra were a couple...a family.

Brouchard made the introduction. "Sara, this is Steve Markovich. He is not only the owner of this hotel, but Barbra's husband."

Stevo said, taking Sara's hand and putting it to his lips, "It is a pleasure to have you with us here at the Dalmatcia."

Confused by the remark, Sara looked from Stevo to Brouchard. Even Barbra was surprised, thinking that Sara would be staying with them at the courtyard.

Stevo said, in an apologetic voice, "We are sorry that we are short of rooms, but hope you don't mind the one we found for you." Taking her by the arm, he led her down the service hall leading to the kitchen and the back door. Barbra and Brouchard followed Stevo and the confused Sara as they passed Stevo's office and Ignatz's room, where just beyond two storage rooms were.

Stevo handed Sara a key, while Barbra, just as surprised as Sara was, stood next to a smiling Brouchard.

Nervously, Sara put the key in the lock. Hearing the click, she pushed the door open.

She let out a scream which she muffled with her hand. There, in what was once a storage room, she saw all of her bedroom furniture. Her canopy bed, the dressing table and the chifferobe with all her dresses, along with her chair were there.

She fell into her chair sobbing. She thought she would have nothing.

Barbra knelt beside Sara, with her arms around her, comforting her new friend. "Oh, Sara", she said, "See, this is just the beginning of your new life."

When everyone was gone and Sara was alone in her room with all the possessions from her former bedroom, she walked around, caressing her dresses and running her hand over the sides of the chifferobe. She had never appreciated them when they were in the house in the Garden District as she did now in the storage room of the hotel.

Stefan Vladeslav walked softly down the hall. He put his ear to Sara's door. It pleased him that he heard her humming. He walked towards the front desk in the lobby. He tore his bidding card from the auction in half, tossing it into a waste basket.

CHAPTER 20

Sara spent a week getting used to living in the Dalmatcia Hotel. It did not bother her that her room was in the back of the hotel near the kitchen.

Sara no longer wore black, though the custom was to be in mourning for at least six months, and even a year. Today, she wore a white long-sleeved blouse and a plaid, green, and brown skirt.

She felt uncomfortable eating in the hotel restaurant, as she had no money to pay for her meals. The server told her not to worry as her meals came with her room.

One morning, joining Mr. Brouchard for breakfast, she asked him, "Who is paying for my room and my meals? And, please don't tell me that it is being paid for with the money from the auction, because I won't believe you."

Brouchard sipped his coffee. When he put the cup down, he thought a moment then decided to tell her the truth. He said, "Steve Markovich is the owner of this hotel. I also have a very small investment in it. We talked about your problem and knowing we had a useable storage room, it was an easy decision to let you have it."

Sara looked at her plate, moving the grits with her fork. She said, "Thank you, Mr. Brouchard. I thought you might be paying for my stay here. I am pleased that I am not costing you any money." She put her fork down. Looking seriously at the banker, she said, "I need to start paying for my stay here."

Brouchard looked surprised. She continued speaking, "I have no money, but, I can work. Surely, Mr. Markovich, can find something worthwhile for me to do. I will clean the rooms. Or, I can work in the gift shop. If nothing else, I can peel potatoes in the kitchen."

Brouchard smiled at Sara. She was a better girl than he had given her credit for. He said, "When we are done with our breakfast, we can find Steve and see what he can offer you."

Just then, Stefan passed their table. He gave them a polite nod on the way to his table.

Sara's lips tightened as she saw him pass by. To Brouchard, she said, "Well, now that the world knows I have no money, he avoids me. He wanted to buy the paddleboat and now doesn't even stop to ask about it. He is so rude! He has not as much as said 'hello' to me."

Her eyes followed him past the tables to a place in the back near a bubbling fountain. She said, "Being a count he ignores me now."

Brouchard lifted a cigar out of his vest pocket. Sara watched as he clipped off the end, all the while looking at her. He lit the cigar, still looking at her. After a couple of puffs on the cigar, he had decided what he would say to her.

"Sara," he began, "I don't know why Stefan is avoiding you. It is none of my business. However," he said, firmly, "you are wrong to think he does not like you or thinks he is better than you."

Sara started to interrupt, but Brouchard stopped her with a raise of his finger. "You see, Sara, you left the house with no clothes. Why Cleona didn't think of that, escapes me."

He took another puff on his cigar, "Stefan heard me tell Steve that I needed to get some clothes out of the house for you. It was Stefan who came forward. He told me to deal with the auctioneer, that he would go with a taxi and get your clothes."

Brouchard saw her eyes widen at what she was hearing. Her lips parted slightly when he said, "Stefan stayed for the auction. He bid on all of your bedroom furniture, not letting anyone outbid him. Then, he hired a truck to bring everything to the hotel and set it up in your room."

Sara's eyes glistened with tears. Starting to rise, she said, "I must go and thank him."

Brouchard grasped her wrist. "Sit down." he demanded. "If Stefan wanted you to know, he would have told you. You say nothing. If and when he wants to have a friendship with you, he will do so."

Sara looked past Brouchard to where Stefan was sitting. She saw him looking at the menu while speaking to the server. She felt so ashamed, remembering how rude she was to him when he was on the boat. Now, she decided it would be better not to approach him. Brouchard was right.

After a while, Brouchard asked, "Sara, are you ready? Have you finished your breakfast?"

Sara nodded yes. As they were leaving the restaurant, Sara looked back at Stefan. He didn't see her. His eyes were fixed on a parrot hanging upside down by its feet on a bar in its cage.

In Stevo's office, Sara glanced around. Of course, just as every visitor in the office did, she noticed the painting of Katya, but said nothing. She listened as Brouchard explained to Stevo that Sara wanted to work, to do anything to repay for her room and food.

Stevo, sitting on his side of the desk, looked at Sara, saying, "It isn't necessary for you to work."

Before he could say anything more, Sara said, "Please let me do something, anything. Don't make me feel as if I am accepting charity."

Stevo looked at Brouchard, whose face was expressionless.

Stevo tapped his fingers on the desktop for a few seconds, then said, "I assume you would have no problem writing receipts or making change if we let you work the gift shop." Then he quickly asked, "Could you be polite to people even if they were not so polite to you?"

Sara looked from Brouchard to Stevo saying, "I am not sure I know what you mean. Why wouldn't people be polite to me?"

Stevo tried to explain, "There are people who will consider you just an employee. Some people will be gracious while others will let you know that you are, to them, just a salesperson."

Sara straightened herself in the wooden-backed chair. She looked at Stevo saying, "Mr. Markovich, I will be as gracious as all the others who work for you. And, yes I can write receipts, add a column of figures, and make change."

"Good." said Stevo. "Can you start today, after a brief tutoring from Anna Mae? You couldn't have asked for a job at a better time. Anna Mae just this morning told me she had to leave to take care of her grandmother."

An hour later, Sara was in the hotel gift shop, wearing the long red dress all the female employees wore. The instructions Anna Mae gave Sara were simple.

Now, with Anna Mae gone, Sara was looking through the shelves to familiarize herself with what was there and to be able to find an item quickly when a customer asked for something in particular.

Sara was especially pleased when Mr. Steve, as he told her to call him, informed her that she would receive a salary. He mentioned to her that, "As recently as a few months ago, a young lady named Danica had the room that you now occupy. She did not pay for her room. We saw to it that she received a salary."

Sara was arranging some perfume bottles on a glass shelf when she heard someone enter the shop. When she straightened up, she was so startled that she nearly lost her balance. She was looking into the dark eyes of Stefan Vladeslav. He had the smallest of smiles as he looked at her.

He had seen her through the shop window so he was not as surprised to see her as she was to see him.

Sara composed herself, asking, "How may I help you?" Had he noticed that her voice cracked, she wondered?

He looked around the shop as he said, "I need some gifts for women. I know that I want the largest box of candy you have." Then he asked, "What perfume would you suggest?"

Sara had no idea what to recommend. She spotted a bottle of Three Flowers Toilet Water by Richard Hudnut. She remembered seeing an ad for it in a magazine. Sara took the bottle and put it on the shelf. She said, trying to sound professional, "This is a very popular scent."

The boxes of candy were all on display on an open shelf. She reached for the largest box of candy.

"Chocolate is a favorite." She said, putting a beautiful, large purple and yellow candy box on the counter.

His back was to her as he studied the assortment of gifts on the shelves against the wall. She took a deep breath to calm herself. *Her first customer was the Count!*

He turned from the wall with a water globe in which was a ship that seemed to move as if in ocean waves. Then, he noticed a red necklace in the glass case. "Add the necklace to my things." Oh, yes, he said, "Give me a couple packs of Fatima cigarettes."

She was aware that her hand trembled slightly as she started writing down his purchases. Stefan noticed. Not wanting to embarrass her, he said, "I don't need a sales slip. Just have it charged to my room."

She found a large enough bag and put everything in it. As she started to hand him the bag, he gave her a small smile, saying, "Thank you, Miss Daniels. Would you mind keeping these here for just a while? I must go to my room right now. I will come for the items, probably within an hour."

She watched him as he went to the elevator near the front desk.

In his room, Stefan had a handheld suitcase given to him by one of the porters. It had been discarded by a hotel guest some time ago.

Stefan didn't want to take his wardrobe trunk on this trip. All he needed were a few casual changes of clothing. From the wall he took down the painting of Barbra. It would go into Stevo's office as Stefan had already asked about storing his things while he was gone. Stevo decided that the wardrobe trunk could be kept in a corner of his office, out of the way.

And, of course, the painting of Barbra would be on the wall next to the one of Katya, the two women he loved the most in his life!

Sara had been so excited and pleased with her first day in the gift shop, that time passed quickly. It was only near five in the afternoon that she noticed Stefan had not come back for his purchases. He had told her he would be back within an hour.

It was while she was removing the cash from the box to put in the cloth bag for the bookkeeper, when Ignatz came into the shop.

"Hello Sara." he said. "I am your neighbor in the room next to yours."

"Hello." Sara replied, not sure why he was in the shop. Before she could ask him if he wanted to buy something, he said, "I am here for Stefan's purchases. He said you were keeping them for him."

She only now realized she had hoped to see Stefan again. She said, "Why did he send you? I expected him hours ago."

Ignatz took the bag she held out to him, saying, "He had some arrangements to make before leaving."

"Leaving? He didn't mention leaving when he was in the shop." said Sara, her voice low and thoughtful. Then she quickly asked, "How well do you know," she didn't want to say Stefan, so she said, "Mr. Vladeslav?"

"I know him very well and for some time. I worked for him in Zagreb and came to America with him a few years ago." As he went out the door, he said, "I must hurry, he will be leaving first thing in the morning!"

Sara, now more intrigued than ever about Stefan, stepped out of the shop to watch Ignatz as he hurried to the elevator to go to Stefan's room.

The next morning, as Sara was preparing to unlock the gift shop to open for the day, she saw Stefan hurrying across the lobby and through the hotel doors, crossing the street to Little Zagreb.

She was very curious about the mysterious and, to her, secretive Count Vladeslav. Sara walked to the entrance of the hotel, stepping outside as the doorman held open the door.

Across the street, in front of Little Zagreb, was the winemaker's wagon. She saw that the heavyset man she had heard called Bronko, was laughing with Stefan at something they had heard.

Both confused and a bit disappointed, Sara saw not only the bag holding the purchases from the gift shop, but a suitcase in the winemaker's wagon.

CHAPTER 21

September 28, 1915

The wagon ride to the Yelich vineyard in the Plaquemines Parish of Louisiana was very pleasant for Stefan. Leaving the city behind, Stefan was delighted by the sights. The countryside smelled of the earth and farms. Yes, he believed he smelled farms.

In the skies, he saw birds one seldom sees in the city. He marveled at the sight of a Swainson's hawk as it circled looking for food. Flocks of geese and ducks were a treat for his eyes. On the ground, in the marshes, he saw herons, a bird new to him.

On the ride, Stefan discovered that he really liked Bronko. Bronko was a simple man, a hardworking man, and proud of what he does. On the ride, listening to Bronko speak of his wife and daughter, of his vineyard, and how long it took to get it established, brought Stefan closer to the man.

Not since coming to America did Stefan feel he was with someone who made him feel so comfortable, so much like the men he remembered working on his father's land, Vladezemla.

Without seeing the Yelich winery, or the vineyards, or the orange groves, Stefan had already decided he wanted to work with Bronko. He asked Bronko questions about possible sales to other cities, which the man dismissed, because of a lack of workers and most of all, lack of funds.

As they rode along the dirt road to the Bronko land, every now and then, Bronko would point out a house in the distance as a house of someone who would help with the grape picking and even with the crushing of the grapes. Bronko told him that usually women would stomp on the grapes with their bare feet, but when there were not enough women men would help with the stomping.

Bronko said, "Tomorrow, I will show you the grape picking baskets. They fit on a man's back and a person walks behind putting the grapes in the basket. We find that a man can carry more on his back that in his hands."

A stronger breeze was felt the closer they got to Bronko's land. He said, "I smell rain."

Stefan was actually excited when he saw the sign over the entry to Bronko's land. It was a wooden sign above the ground the width of the road. Before they drove the horses under the sign, Stefan saw the blue, painted words, YELICH WINERY. Around the name were painted pictures of red grape clusters.

Bronko drove the horses to the back of a simple, wooden house. Behind the house was a stable, and near it was a barn. Stefan could see a young girl herding the chickens and some ducks into the barn, as she too, was anticipating rain.

Bronko's wife, Marina, came out of the house to greet her husband. She was surprised to see a stranger. Bronko said, "Marina, we need to make room for our new friend, Stefan Vladeslav. He will be with us a few days."

To Stefan, Bronko said, "Go in the house with Marina. I will put the horses in the barn." He called to his daughter gathering the chickens, "Yaga, come quick. Help me get the wagon in the barn."

Stefan had the bag of gifts in one hand and the suitcase in the other as Marina showed him into the house. From the back entrance, they entered into the kitchen.

Stefan looked around the kitchen. It was as if he were home in his family house. On the wooden counter with an indoor pump for water, was a large bowl of onions and lettuce. Alongside he saw some heads of garlic.

He saw, on the tablecloth, some freshly made noodles drying. From the wood stove, came the smell of bread baking.

Marina pulled out a wooden chair, she said, "Put your things here. I have coffee. Sit down. Bronko will be in soon."

Stefan was very comfortable in the kitchen as he was with Marina. She only spoke Croatian. It was not the exact dialect that he spoke, being from the Zagreb area and she from Dalmatcia, but they easily understood each other.

Marina had her head covered with a babushka, tied at the back of her neck. Her skirt and long-sleeved blouse were of heavy, blue cotton. Over this, she had a full-bibbed apron to protect her clothing.

On the wood stove, Stefan could smell chicken cooking in a pot.

Bronko came in, pulling off his cap. He said, "That wind is really picking up. I think we are going to have a big storm. Even the animals are restless."

Bronko put his arm around the shoulders of his dark-haired daughter, who looked to be about 13 or 14 years old. She was slender and not very tall.

"This is our Yaga." said Bronko with pride. "She is such a hard worker."

Just then, the kitchen door opened with a bang, the wind hitting it against the wall. Bronko's sister, Alta, hurried into the house, escaping the growing fierceness of the wind.

She stopped, startled at the sight of Stefan in the kitchen. She composed herself and gave him a dazzling smile, believing he had come to see her.

Alta ran her hand over her windblown hair and walked toward Stefan, who was seated at the kitchen table. "How nice of you to come and visit us." she almost purred. She was in a long-skirted green dress.

"Hello." said Stefan, nodding politely. He looked away from her and asked Marina, "Are you going to mix the noodles with the chicken I smell cooking?"

The stunned look on Alta's face at being ignored by Stefan did not go unnoticed by her brother, who smiled, very pleased. Now he was sure that Stefan wanted to learn about winemaking. In the back of his mind, he had wondered if Stefan, like so many other men, really wanted to accept Alta's offered charms.

Alta stood speechless, staring at Stefan, who did not look at her, but continued his conversation with Marina about the food.

Bronko's smile did not go unnoticed by his annoyed sister. Without a word, she went to the bedroom she shared with her niece.

Bronko placed three glasses on a small side table, as the kitchen table had the noodles on it. He filled the glasses with wine, one for Stefan, one for Marina, and one for himself. They raised their glasses saying, "Nazdravlje."

Stefan picked up the bag of gifts which he handed to Marina. "You decide who gets these." he said. "You get to pick first."

Marina was torn between choosing the perfume or the necklace of red beads. She finally chose the beads. Yaga was very excited and she was sent to the bedroom calling Alta, telling her there were gifts.

Curious, but still annoyed with her brother, Alta came into the kitchen. She gave Stefan a friendly look, but it wasn't her usual flirty one.

"Look," said Marina. "You may pick out a gift first, since you are older than Yaga."

It didn't take Alta but a moment to take the Richard Hudnut Three Flowers perfume. She gave Stefan a nice smile saying, "Hvala...Thank you."

Yaga was thrilled to get the largest gift of all, the box of chocolate candy. Left was the water globe with the moving ship in it. Stefan took the globe handing it to the young Yaga, who was thrilled. "Za tebe...for you." he said.

The meal was ready and the table was set. It was darker than usual for this time of day with dark clouds on the horizon. The menacing wind continued with the threat of rain.

The meal was pleasant and the food was very good. Alta didn't want to flirt or tease Stefan. There was something different about him. What's more, for the first time, she didn't want to behave as she had in the past with men. She had been easy and available. Tonight, she wanted to be the nice sister of Bronko Yelich. What's more, it pleased her when she heard that Stefan would be staying a few days.

Alta's almost ladylike demeanor did not go unnoticed by her brother. It pleased him that she was behaving. He liked Stefan and he hoped there was the chance of a partnership.

Young Yaga had gone to bed, taking her treasured box of chocolate candy and the glass globe with her.

The house did not have sitting room, as they did not entertain anywhere but in the kitchen. It was decided that Stefan would sleep on the cot in Bronko's room where he kept his business accounts and plans for the wine. He didn't call it an office, but that is what the room really was.

The mood in the kitchen was full of friendly warmth. Bronko knew that he liked Stefan and they would work well together, if it came to that.

Bronko said, "Tomorrow, I take you to the barn where we age the wine and later to the vineyards. So much I want you to see."

Stefan offered his open cigarette case to Bronko, who took one of the Fatima cigarettes. Alta remembered seeing that beautiful gold case at Little Zagreb.

Along with the wine bottle on the center of the table, was a plate of flat squares of dough with something Stefan did not recognize. Marina laughed when she saw the questioning look on Stefan's face. She said, "This is what we do with the grapes

Bronko rejects for his wine. I put the grapes on a screen and leave them out in the sun to dry and shrivel like you see. I use them in baking."

Stefan took a square and bit into it. "This is delicious." He said, after his first taste of raisins.

Alta felt so comfortable with Stefan. She didn't want to flirt or try and seduce him. She liked him. He wasn't like most of the men she seduced and did not respect.

The mood in the simple kitchen was warm and comforting. A feeling of strong friendship enveloped the four people around the table.

Noticing the hanging oil lamp start to sway made the four of them look up. A sound of something crashing in the yard made them all jump up.

What had begun as a weak tropical storm some seven days earlier in the Gulf of Mexico, was now a 125-mile-an-hour wind that instantly tore the Yelich house apart, flinging the occupants out into what would be known as the worst hurricane since 1856.

Plaquemines Parish was covered with 15 feet of water. The oyster beds were destroyed. Some 200 deaths were reported, with many of the missing never found.

Stefan Vladeslav was gone, as was all of the Yelich family.

CHAPTER 22

As a rule, Stevo would go his Canal Street home each evening. Last night, he stayed at the hotel because there was a banquet in the men's lounge along with an engagement party in the ballroom. With events like these, Stevo liked to be available to oversee that everything was properly taken care of. It was late when he stretched out on a cot in his office.

It was about 5:30 in the morning of September 29 that Stevo heard sounds such as he had never heard before. The sound of the screaming wind and flying objects crashing outdoors awakened him in a panic. He had no idea what was happening. He had not undressed the night before, so he was in his shirt and trousers, on the cot in his office.

As he sat up, he was sure he saw a young tree, roots and all, flying past his office window. Confused and in fear, he ran to his window in time to see some bird cages from the outdoor dining area being tossed like paper in the wind.

Running shoeless out of his office, he saw the night clerk in shock staring at the entry door. Stevo ran to the front desk in time to see the entry doors of the hotel blown open. The uncontrollable wind and rain swept into the lobby, pushing aside tables and moving some chairs.

Ignatz was behind Stevo, barefoot, wearing only an undershirt and his trousers. Seeing the water pouring into the hotel, Ignatz said, "Sveti Isus...Holy Jesus." With fear in his voice, he asked, "What is happening?"

"I don't know." Stevo was shouting over the roar of the wind and the sound of breaking glass.

Sara, terror in her eyes, ran to Stevo and Ignatz. Frightened, she wrapped her arms around Ignatz. Feeling her trembling body, he held on to her.

Brouchard appeared from the staircase. He said, "The elevator is not working. Also, the phones are out." He was shouting because of the howling sound from the storm. "It's a dammed hurricane. I can tell it is a bad one."

Stevo shouted back to Brouchard, "I have to go to the courtyard. I need to be with the family."

Just then, water started to run down the stairway.

Sara was sobbing. The sound of wood being torn from buildings could be heard along with people screaming.

In his bare feet, Stevo ran to the front of the hotel. The doors were not only blown open, but blown off their hinges. Stevo stepped into the rain, which felt like pellets against his face. He started to go to Canal Street. He had to be with his family. He needed to know they were alright! He had to be there to help them!

The rain and wind with loose flying boards and debris sent Stevo back into the hotel, where the water was rising on the lobby floor.

Unable to leave and losing track of time, Sara, Ignatz, Brouchard, and Stevo sat perched atop stacked lobby chairs behind the hotel's front desk. When the clerk had disappeared, no one knew. From their mound of chairs, they watched, sick with fear and worry at the rising water level in the lobby.

Stevo could hear calls for help from the above floors. He was sick that he could do nothing for his guests. Every now and then was heard a crashing sound, which must have been something torn from a building landing outside.

Brouchard was not doing so well. At his age, the stress and fear for his granddaughter, Kate, his adopted family of Barbra, Cleona, Bobo, and little Joso, made him weak. Then there was his home where his sister lived. Would it be there when this assault of nature would be over? He thought of Asa, once a childhood friend, now his servant. Dear God, he thought, take care of those I love.

Meanwhile, at the courtyard, Barbra and the children huddled in fear in the main house. The phone didn't work and Barbra had no idea if Steve was safe. She wished he were with them, she was aware that no one was on the street.

Barbra had no idea of the time. There was constant rain, with frightening sounds of the hurricane, taking with it the tops of buildings while flooding the streets with a river of water.

When part of the roof of the main house was ripped off, allowing the pelting rain to attack them, Barbra, with the crying Kate and Joso, along with baby Gabriella in her arms, started, almost blindly, to descend the stairs.

Fighting the rain, Cleona had come from her house. She was on the stairs taking the baby into her arms, leading the way out of the house, to hers across the courtyard. The house she stayed in was not as high as the main house, so the dangerous wind seemed to pass over it.

In Cleona's house, she tried to find some dry towels and even blankets with which to wrap the crying children.

A part of the roof of Bobo's carriage house was carried away by the dangerous winds. He tried to find a safe place on the stairs leading to the barn below. The barn doors swung open in the wind and rain.

The next morning, Thursday, the people of New Orleans, dazed and frightened, looked out at the devastation. The sun shined over the city. Residents were stunned by the effects of the wind. More than 25,000 structures suffered serious damage. Some eleven or more churches lost their steeples. Close to the Dalmatcia Hotel and the Little Zagreb was the French Market, where the pavilions were leveled.

Streets were damaged and light poles were on the ground, broken in half.

Stevo was sick with worry about his family, while Barbra also worried about him. There were no phones, no taxis, and no carriages to be seen.

Stevo ran through the ankle deep water in the streets, hurrying to his home and his loved ones. When he reached Canal Street, he saw Bobo leaning against the still-standing wall of the courtyard.

Bobo was crying. Seeing Stevo he wailed, "She is gone. My Cleona is gone."

Stevo clutched his hand to his chest. Not Cleona, Oh, God. Not Cleona.

Bobo waived his hand, pointing across the street. There lay his beloved horse, Cleona, named as a joke after his cousin Cleona.

In the battering rain, when the doors of the barn had blown open, the frightened horse had run through the yard out onto the street. A falling lamp pole landed on the horse, killing her instantly.

Stevo gave Bobo a sympathetic pat on the shoulder as he passed him going into the yard. He saw water slowly flowing out of the yard into the street.

He was shocked to see part of the roof from the main house now in scattered pieces in the courtyard. It was the same when Stevo looked at Bobo's carriage house. It was with great relief he saw that the small house now used by Cleona and once belonging to Miss Kara and Brouchard was still standing with its roof intact.

Little Kate was the first to see Stevo. She came splashing through the water throwing her arms around him when she reached him, clinging to him, making it impossible for him to move. She was sobbing as she clung to him.

Barbra came running across the patio to Steve. "My Dearest." She kept repeating. Her arms were around him, but she couldn't get very close because Kate would not let go of her Uncle Steve.

Cleona stood in the doorway with tears streaming down her cheeks. With one hand she held Joso's little hand and with the other, she held Gabriella. The events of the day before had frightened the little brown-haired Joso so much, that he would not let go of Cleona's hand. He felt safe with her.

After a while, Barbra and Stevo went up soggy stairs, dripping of water, to where they lived in the main house. Their living area was soaked and the furniture tossed about. Items that had been on tables or the desk were scattered on the floor. Their bedroom, with the window overlooking the courtyard facing the patio, was also tossed about. The bedding, curtains, and clothing, like everything else, was drenched.

In front of the window, Stevo took Barbra in his arms. It was where he often watched Barbra at the patio table, when she lived there alone. They clung to each other, grateful they still had one another and their small family. They kissed in a way they had never before. Words could never describe what they felt now. Their love had been tested in a way neither could have believed possible.

At the hotel, there was no dry wood with which to make a fire. The fire pit in the outdoor eating area was useless as everything was wet.

Patrons of the hotel wandered about dazed, wearing wet clothing. Some were still in bathrobes. They were looking for food or coffee. Most of all, they were looking for someone to tell them what to do, where to go, how to get out of New Orleans.

It would be many days before electricity could be restored. The streetcar barn was totally destroyed, but then, so were many of the city's streetcar tracks.

The people who ventured out onto the streets were either looking for a family member, or hoping to find food.

CHAPTER 23

Chicago, September 30, 1915

"Michael! Michael, get up!" Coralynn screamed at her still sleeping husband.

Michael DuKane nearly fell as he hurried out of bed, thinking the Drake Hotel was on fire from the way Coralynn was screaming.

He stood bewildered, looking at Coralynn, who was staring at him, her eyes wild.

Annoyed, he let out a sigh before saying, "I swear Coralynn, if you woke me up because you saw another spider, I'll make you sleep on the floor."

She couldn't speak. He saw the tears streaming down her cheeks.

Now fully awake, realizing something serious was the matter, he put his arms around her saying, "My God, Coralynn, what is wrong?"

She stood before him, trembling. Her hand was out stretched holding the morning paper which had been delivered with the breakfast tray.

Michael looked from Coralynn to the newspaper. The bold headlines read:

HURRICANE SWEEPS OVER NEW ORLEANS
Hurricane Kills Ten People
Causing Property Loss in the Millions of Dollars

"Oh, My God! Dear God!" repeated Michael. "We have to call to find out what has happened and if they are alright."

Michael picked up his robe, unable to put it on while grabbing the phone. He didn't realize he was shouting when he said into the phone, "I need long distance. I need to call New Orleans."

The hotel telephone operator told him she would call as soon as she could make the connection to a New Orleans operator.

Putting the phone receiver in its cradle, Michael stared at Coralynn, whose face was colorless. For several moments, they just looked at one another. Without speaking, they were in each other's arms, holding onto one another.

After a bit, Michael went into the bathroom. He splashed handfuls of cold water onto his face, wetting his beard.

When he returned to their comfortable hotel room, Coralynn was pouring coffee for them both. She pointed to the dome-covered food dishes, asking, "Do want some breakfast?"

Now in his blue and yellow paisley-printed bathrobe, he shook his head saying, "No, Lynnie. I don't think I can eat anything."

Lynnie had become his affectionate name for Coralynn. What had started out almost as a marriage for appearances was now one of true love and affection.

The ringing of the phone startled them both. Michael grabbed the phone, "Hello, hello, New Orleans operator?" he said.

"Sorry Sir. This is the hotel operator. We have been informed that any communication with New Orleans is impossible at this time."

Michael, stunned, felt a knot in the pit of his stomach.

"Sir...Sir?" The hotel operator said, "Sir is there another call you would like to make at this time?"

Coralynn put her coffee cup down. She had never seen Michael look so ill, so...so frightened.

In a voice Coralynn hardly recognized, she heard Michael say, "No, operator, no, nothing more."

Slowly, Michael replaced the receiver on the phone's cradle. Without a word, he slowly, with what looked to Coralynn like great effort, Michael came to the table and sat down.

"Well," she asked, 'What did the operator say? When will the call to New Orleans go through?"

Michael slowly turned his head. He looked at his Lynnie, dreading the words he had to say. "There is no communication available to or with New Orleans."

For a moment, Coralynn let the words sink in. She stared at Michael for what seemed a long time. When she spoke, it was in a low and serious voice. She said, "We are getting on a train and we are going home. I need to know if we have lost anyone. Or, if anyone is hurt and needs us."

Tears were streaming down her face, "Michael, I need to know!"

Michael sighed deeply. He took a sip of his cooled coffee, wondering if the agreement with Marshall Fields and Mr. White was binding.

The phone rang, startling them both. Michael snatched up the receiver. He anxiously said, "Hello? Hello?"

Mr. White's voice said, "Hello, Michael. I just read the paper. How are you and Coralynn?"

Coralynn's hopeful look disappeared when she heard Michael say, "Good Morning, Mr. White. We saw the paper and have tried to call our family in New Orleans, but there is no available communication, or so the phone operator said."

"Yes,' said Mr. White, "I tried calling people I know there and couldn't get through."

Michael paused, asking, "Do you think I would be breaking any agreement with the store if I left for New Orleans? Coralynn and I are hoping to take a train."

There was a long silence on the phone line. Michael was sure he was in an unbreakable agreement with Marshall Fields.

"Michael," said Mr. White, "I have already looked into it for you."

Pleased, Michael said, "Thank you! Thank you so very much."

"Michael…" The tone of Mr. White's voice disturbed Michael. He sensed something was wrong. "Michael," Mr. White continued, "You can't take a train. The rails leading to New Orleans have been washed away."

Michael didn't go to the Fields gallery that day, or for three more days.

He and Coralynn were ill with worry. It was as if they were in mourning. They read any scrap of news they found in the papers and listened to the radio hoping for good news.

It was good they didn't know of all the destruction of the hurricane or they would have felt worse, if that were possible.

With many of its structures already more than a century old, the damage was extensive. It would take a while to restore the beauty of the city.

CHAPTER 24

All of New Orleans was in pain, as so much needed to be repaired. Not everyone was willing to believe the city would be normal again.

Almost everyone was in different degrees of shock after the hurricane.

It took weeks and sometimes months for power to be restored in the city. The pumps did not empty the city of water as quickly as hoped. Some parts of New Orleans had water depths of seven feet.

Everyone did whatever was necessary to try and make the best of the chaos in the city. Brouchard and Sara tried to help the guests in the hotel, but it was not easy, as there was no dry wood with which to heat water for coffee and for a long time there was no clean water to drink.

Boats traveling along the Louisiana waterways passed many rafts with desperate people, with nothing but the tattered clothes they wore.

The people on the rafts would cry out, begging for food. Food was thrown from the boats to those who were so grateful for even a bit of bread.

The boat captains, who had for many years traveled the waters of Louisiana, had never witnessed the heartbreaking scenes of devastation and helplessness they now encountered.

In time, supplies found their way to the desperate people in Louisiana and New Orleans.

Mr. White, in Chicago along with Michael DuKane and Coralynn, bought supplies to send to New Orleans by any means they could find.

Mr. White called anyone he knew through his business connections in the hopes that they could send or find ways to deliver help to those he knew in New Orleans.

With the streetcar rails damaged and Bobo's horse dead, it was two weeks before Brouchard found a man with a horse-drawn wagon willing to drive to Brouchard's family home up on Chartres Street.

Brouchard's heart nearly stopped when he saw what was left of the stunning house built by his grandfather in the mid 1800s. The house appeared to be just so much rubble.

Fighting back tears along with his heart full of fear, he told the wagon driver, "Stay here until I come back. It looks as if I have to go around to the back."

Brouchard could feel his eyes filling with tears. His family home...it was gone! At the back of the house nothing was left of the beautiful gardens.

Brouchard made his way across the terrace, stepping over the broken pottery and damaged cement statues strewn about.

The glass doors leading from the terrace into the house were gone. What greeted the old man looked as if an explosion had destroyed the house.

Brouchard was in shock as he tried to move some broken bookshelves so he could make his way past an upturned table.

"Who's there?" demanded a gruff voice. "What you doin' here?"

Brouchard's heart gave a leap when he recognized his childhood friend and the man who oversaw the running of the house.

"Asa? Asa, where are you? It's me, Harold."

Asa, wearing soiled clothing, stepped out from behind a stack of tumbled and scattered rubble.

Harold carefully made his way to the Black man he loved like a brother. The man he grew up with as a child. Asa learned to read alongside Harold, while working the land owned by the Brouchard family.

The two men wrapped their arms around each other, tears falling on both their cheeks.

"I was hoping you would find us." said Asa, as the men held onto each other.

Brouchard let go of Asa, looking around, asking, "Evalynn, where is Evalynn? Is she alright?"

Brouchard didn't like the look on Asa's face. He asked, "What's wrong? Is she hurt?"

Asa led the way through the rubble to a far corner of what had been a ballroom. There, an area had been cleared with a makeshift resting place for Brouchard's sister.

Brouchard started to hurry to his sister, when Asa, taking his arm, stopped the old banker.

"She won't know you." said Asa. "She hasn't said one word since the hurricane hit this house. At first, she screamed and screamed...then she got quiet. This is how she is now."

All the mean and nasty things Evalynn had done and said in the past, when her husband was arrested for stealing from the bank, no longer mattered. His once beautiful, strong sister was now just a frail, thin body resting on soiled pillows.

Brouchard knelt beside his sister. "Oh, Evalynn...Dear God, Evalynn."

Asa watched as his dear friend sobbed, holding his sister's hand.

After a while, Brouchard stood up, wiping his eyes with the sleeve of his shirt. He looked around the rubble, wondering if anything could be saved.

To Asa, he said, "Go out front and tell the man in the wagon, to make room for some things we are bringing out."

In the tossed chaos that had once been his own room, Brouchard found his Chinese teakwood chest damaged on the floor. The water had soaked it and popped out some of the wooden inlayed marquetry.

In one of the hidden drawers he found a velvet box. Inside, he found the family jewelry he had hidden from Evalynn, who would have given it to her worthless husband.

Holding the box of valuable baubles, Brouchard chuckled ruefully.

He said aloud to himself, "If only this were food."

CHAPTER 25

The wagon with Asa, Evalynn, and Brouchard drove into the courtyard, stopping in front of the house where Cleona stayed. It was the house that Brouchard bought for the love of his life, his beautiful octoroon, Miss Kara, who was also Little Kate's grandmother.

Asa was the first out of the wagon. He looked around the courtyard and could see that it had once been a very beautiful place. The large main house still showed damage as did the carriage house.

Brouchard used the one metal step as he descended from the wagon. He motioned for the wagon driver to stay where he was.

As always, Barbra and the children were on the patio, enjoying the warm sun. On the tables were assorted washed clothing, bedding, and towels drying.

Their lives were not normal and would not be for a very long time.

Cleona sensed something was unusual with this visit.

She approached Brouchard saying, "Hello, Mr. Brouchard."

Looking at Asa, she asked, "Is something the matter? I thought you would be at the bank or the hotel."

Kate also sensed something was different about this arrival. She remembered Asa from the one time she and her Uncle Steve had brunch at the house on Chartres Street. She remembered that she did not like grandpère's sister. Kate did not run to her grandfather and wrap her arms around him. This time she only stood back watching.

Brouchard took Cleona's elbow and led her away from the patio, farther into the courtyard so they would not be heard.

The children and Barbra silently watched them as they walked away.

Asa was a little nervous. He stood in front of Barbra saying, "I am Asa, Mr. Harold and I have been friends since we were young boys. I take care of his house." He paused, "That is, I took care of it while it was a house. It is pretty much gone now."

"Hello, Asa. I am Barbra." She motioned with hand toward a chair, "Won't you sit down?"

Concerned about Brouchard's conversation with Cleona, Asa said, "Thank you, Ma'am. Not just yet."

Now away from everyone, Cleona asked, "You want something, don't you? What do you want?"

Brouchard cleared his throat, "I need your help. I really do."

Cleona said, "You know that you only need to ask and I will do it." She studied his troubled face, waiting for him to speak.

He said, "Cleona…Cleona, my house is pretty much gone." He nodded towards Asa saying, "Asa is my oldest and closest friend."

This surprised Cleona, as Asa was a Black man and she assumed that Mr. Steve was Brouchard's closest friend.

Brouchard continued, "My sister is in the wagon. Something has happened to her. She doesn't know me and…and she doesn't know anything. She doesn't speak."

Cleona could sense what was coming next. She said, "You want me to take your sister in?"

Brouchard said, "You won't have to care for her. Asa will take care of her. They just need somewhere to stay."

Cleona admired Mr. Brouchard. Also, it was his house she was living in, just as if it were her own.

"I will do anything for you. You know there is room. Asa can have the maid's room off the kitchen."

Looking around she asked, "Where is your sister?"

Brouchard waived to Asa, pointing to the wagon, as he and Cleona walked back to the patio.

Asa was a strong man and Evalynn had become thinner since the hurricane changed their lives. Asa picked up Evalynn, following Cleona, who led the way to an upstairs back bedroom, the bedroom where Kate's mother gave birth to her and where she died that same night.

Asa came out of the house alone. Cleona stayed upstairs with Evalynn. She looked at the frail, unresponsive woman. For just a brief moment, Cleona wondered how this Southern woman would treat her, if she could speak.

After Asa brought in what little he had brought from the Chartres Street house, Brouchard told Asa to sit down at a table in the kitchen. He wanted to speak with Asa in private. It did, however, surprise him that Kate stayed at Barbra's side.

Brouchard and his friend, Asa, sat across from one another. Brouchard was the first to speak. He said, "My friend, I know this is going to be a challenge for you, living away from what has been your home since we were boys."

Asa reached out and grasped Brouchard's hand, saying, "Harold, we do what we have to do and we do the best we can. I will try and not be a bother to the people here."

Brouchard looked fondly at his friend saying, "Asa. I think of all these people as my family. You will find that they are good and kind."

Cleona appeared. She said, "Excuse me for interrupting. Your sister is asleep." She turned to Asa, "I can find you a little to eat. We don't have much, but something is better than nothing."

Asa's eyes brightened. "Thank you, Miss Cleona." he said. "We ate the last of what was from last year's canning jars that didn't get busted up two days ago."

Brouchard stood up, saying, "I better pay the wagon man and get back to the hotel."

To Cleona he said, "Take good care of my friend, Asa. He is like a brother to me."

Outside at the patio table, he gave Barbra a kiss, patted Joso on the head, and sitting at the table, he spread his arms wide so that Kate could hug her grandfather.

She came to him, almost shyly. Gone was the strong-willed and confident Little Kate. The hurricane had frightened the young girl to her very core. She realized that in one day, she could have lost everyone she cared for and everything that was part of her young life.

CHAPTER 26

About three months after the hurricane, Brouchard was still staying at the hotel with his windows boarded up, waiting for replacement. He felt it was certain that Stefan Vladeslav and the Yelich family had perished in the hurricane. He opened Stefan's private box at the bank to go through the papers. The first item he found was a hand-written paper folded in half. At the bottom he recognized the stamped seal of the bank and the signature of one of his assistants. He was looking at Stefan's will. By the date, Brouchard determined it had been written some time after he had been with Barbra at the Canal Street courtyard. Brouchard let out a deep breath as he realized the will left everything to Barbra.

After finding the will, he went to the courtyard on Canal Street, where he found Barbra sorting through a wash tub of kitchen items to see what could be kept and what to discard. Kate was rocking baby Gabriella in a makeshift swing made from a blanket hanging from a tree limb, while Joso played with stones building houses. Cleona and Virgine were at the far end of the courtyard, washing bedding.

When Kate saw her grandfather, she immediately ran to him, wrapping her arms around his waist saying, "How nice to see you. Can you stay?" After hugs and kisses, Brouchard said, "Kate, dear, I must have a talk with Barbra. After that I will be all yours." Kate looked from Brouchard to Barbra and sensed something serious was happening. Oh, how she wished she could sit with them and listen!

Just then, Stevo came into the courtyard, surprising Barbra. Kate, sensing the visit of her grandfather and Uncle Steve was an important one, instinctively stayed with Gabriella.

"I came as soon as I got your phone message." said Stevo, as he kissed a very surprised Barbra.

Brouchard said, "Let's sit at the table."

Barbra and Stevo looked at one another, not sure what could be so important that Stevo had to leave the damaged hotel and Brouchard his bank at this time of day.

There was a time when Cleona would be offering refreshments, but times were different now.

Stevo sat next to Barbra, across from Brouchard. Seeing the serious look on the old banker's face, Stevo, reaching for Barbra's hand, asked, "What is it Harold?"

Brouchard looked from Barbra to Stevo. Clearing his throat, he began, "Stefan Vladeslav was not very liked or even accepted by us." He saw the confused looks on the faces of Barbra and Stevo. He hesitated long enough for Stevo to ask, "Harold, what are you trying to say?"

"I opened Stefan's box at the bank this morning." said Brouchard, as he again cleared his throat.

"So?" Stevo was getting impatient. It was not like Brouchard to hesitate this way when he had something to say.

"He was a wealthy man." said Brouchard. Before Stevo could interrupt again, Brouchard said quickly, "And, he left everything in his will to Barbra."

Both Barbra and Stevo stared at Brouchard, speechless.

CHAPTER 27

One year after the hurricane, and the evening before the grand opening of the new and more elegant Dalmatcia Hotel, everyone was gathered for a private celebration.

When the shock of receiving the inheritance from Stefan wore off, Barbra shared the money with Tomo and Stevo, so they could repair and rebuild what had been damaged.

The main house at Canal Street now had a wrought iron balcony on two sides of the house instead of only on the front. Bobo's carriage house was repaired and Asa shared the living quarters with him. Brouchard's sister passed away, so now, Cleona had the small house to herself once again.

With the money and bonds left by Stefan to Barbra, beautiful furnishings were trucked into New Orleans from nearby states to make the Dalmatcia even more beautiful than before.

The hotel doorman, again in a red uniform and red top hat, stood watch to insure this event remained a private party.

The main floor of the hotel, with lovely Art Nouveau furnishings, was a room filled with love. Everyone there was so much a part of one another's lives that they were as a family. Brouchard looked at all the guests, who were bound to one another by a language and a history that the old banker envied. He looked at Tomo and Stevo, like father and son, or even brothers. Beautiful Barbra, not a Croatian, but born in Germany. There was wonderful, loyal, hard-working Ignatz. To Brouchard's surprise, Michael DuKane, Coralynn, and even Mr. White from Marshall Fields were all here for this special event.

Cleona, Bobo, and even Asa were part of this group…this family. Missing was Virgine, who had left to care for her own family. Little Kate, feeling so grown up, looked after Joso and Gabriella.

The newest member of this gathering was Sara. Brouchard was now her father figure, as was Stevo.

This was a happy gathering, with much kissing and laughter. They all had a strong feeling for one another.

Sadly what was missing was the Yelich wine, and especially, Bronko Yelich, himself, who certainly would have been invited to such an important occasion for one of his clients. Instead, there was Jamaican wine.

Asa carried the trays of wine glasses to the guests, while Cleona and Stevo held the wine bottles.

When it came time for a toast, Tomo raised his glass, saying, "To a better New Orleans."

Stevo stood next to Barbra, his arm around her. He raised his glass in a toast. He said, "To Count Stefan Vladislav."

THE END

9 781644 385180